Hi, Charlotte,

Thanks for your la— ——— *family. It's been so* ——— *time to write, but I'm not complaining. The B and B's still full most of the time, and if that's not enough to keep me busy, the upcoming Cajun musical festival is. Local businesses are planning to have display booths on the opera house grounds, so I'll be doing something to promote La Petite Maison.*

You'd be surprised at the caliber of Indigo's few businesses. There's a woman here named Loretta Castille who's started up a bakery specializing in artisanal breads. She's been supplying La Petite Maison with all our baked goods and they rival anything you can find in New Orleans—everything from cranberry-walnut muffins to olive bread. Loretta's great. She's a single mom with a really precocious daughter, Zara. I'll miss them both once my probation's up and I move on. Until then, I'll keep putting all my energy into La Petite Maison so Grand-mère Celeste and the rest of you will believe that I really have turned my life around. I'll never get so much as a parking ticket for the rest of my life.

Love to you all,

Luc

Dear Reader,

When Hurricane Katrina hit, like everyone else, I felt just awful. Not only did hundreds of people lose their lives and thousands more their homes, but one of my favorite cities was changed irrevocably. Since I'm a Texan, Louisiana is my close neighbor, and I've been there more than a dozen times—trips with my parents when I was a little girl, wild weekends when I was in college, writers conferences and camping trips as an adult. My husband proposed to me in New Orleans.

But it's not just New Orleans. The Louisiana swamps hold a strange appeal for me—all that Spanish moss, funky Cajun cafés and little shacks deep in the woods, and plantation homes. A few years ago, I bicycled across southern Louisiana and saw the state from a whole new perspective.

I want to hold tight to my memories and think of Louisiana and New Orleans as I knew it—which is how I depicted the area in this book. When I make mention of the hurricane damage, I emphasize the resilient spirit of Louisianans, and the rebuilding. I hope that by the time you read this book, my predictions are reality.

Sincerely,

Kara Lennox

KARA LENNOX
A Second Chance

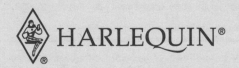

HARLEQUIN®

TORONTO • NEW YORK • LONDON
AMSTERDAM • PARIS • SYDNEY • HAMBURG
STOCKHOLM • ATHENS • TOKYO • MILAN • MADRID
PRAGUE • WARSAW • BUDAPEST • AUCKLAND

Recycling programs
for this product may
not exist in your area.

ISBN-13: 978-0-373-18914-4

A SECOND CHANCE

Printed in U.S.A.

Kara Lennox is a bestselling author who has written more than fifty contemporary romance novels. She lives in Texas with her husband, also a writer, and a small menagerie. Her ever-changing hobbies include cross-country bicycling, metal-detecting, bird-watching and mosaics; most recently she's taken up cooking. Kara has earned her living as an art director, a fitness instructor, an advertising copywriter, an actress and a blackjack dealer, but she prefers writing to just about anything.

CHAPTER ONE

THE SUN WASN'T UP YET, but Luc Carter had been out of bed for an hour. His bed-and-breakfast guests, a bird-watching couple from Washington, D.C., were planning an early-morning trip up the Bayou Teche to try to spot an ivory-billed woodpecker, and Luc had promised them a full-course breakfast at 7:00 a.m.

He didn't mind getting up early. He liked the quiet hours before his guests were awake—before anyone in the whole town of Indigo, Louisiana, was awake, except maybe for Loretta.

Loretta. He had to stop thinking about her. But how could he stop thinking about her when he saw her almost every morning? Loretta Castille baked the most delicious breads and muffins in all of Louisiana, and she brought them fresh each day to La Petite Maison B and B. Some guests claimed the breads were what brought them back to Indigo again and again.

He checked the frittata in the oven, then returned to squeezing oranges for fresh juice. Coffee with chicory perked on the stove, sending a delectable scent throughout the two-hundred-year-old Creole cottage he'd spent the last year restoring with his own hands.

As he mixed fresh strawberries and walnuts into a bowl of yogurt, he kept his eye on the front window.

Loretta would be arriving any minute with her bountiful basket. How sad that the high point of his day usually occurred before breakfast.

As the sky began to glow pink, then orange, the familiar *chug-chug* of Loretta's old Volvo station wagon carried through the screen door.

On time, as usual. She was never late for a delivery. Loretta worked day and night to make a go of her baking business. It was hard to maintain any business in a small town like Indigo, but people managed.

Luc passed through the screen door and went out to the porch to greet Loretta. She was always in a hurry, with a long list of customers from St. Martinville to New Iberia awaiting her breads, and she appreciated not having to hunt him down.

The station wagon pulled to a stop, and before Loretta could even cut the engine, the passenger door opened and a red-headed, four-foot bundle of energy burst out of the car and straight for him. The child— Loretta's nine-year-old daughter, Zara—looked as if she were going to run straight into him. But she skidded to a stop a few feet shy of Luc, as if she'd suddenly remembered that she wasn't the type of child to go around hugging people.

And she wasn't.

"Hi."

"Hi, yourself, gorgeous." She was beautiful, with a mischievous, pixie face, thick, wavy red hair and warm hazel eyes that would break a lot of hearts one day. She looked heart-stoppingly like her mother. "You're up awful early for a Saturday morning."

"I wanted to see the bird-watchers. Mama says you have bird-watchers all the way from Washington staying with you."

Zara was the most curious child Luc had ever encountered. Not that he'd known many children, other than his little cousin, Rosie, in New Orleans.

"The bird-watchers aren't up yet," Luc told Zara. "But you're not missing much. They look just like ordinary people, I promise." Luc watched Loretta emerge from her car with a cheery wave. She looked fantastic, as always, in a pair of tight, faded jeans and a gauzy blue shirt, her spiky red hair sticking out every which way, as if she hadn't combed it since rolling out of bed.

He liked that look, though he didn't care to speculate on why. Dangerous territory, thinking about Loretta and bed.

"Is anyone else staying with you?" Zara asked, peeking past him to the doorway, perhaps hoping to catch a glimpse of some exotic guest.

"Uh-huh. Two more couples, one from Shreveport and one from Houston."

"Are they interesting?"

"The couple from Shreveport are pretty fun. Newlyweds." Luc lowered his voice to a conspiratorial whisper. "But the ones from Houston—snooty. Nothing's good enough for them. I had to get them a different kind of soap, and a different kind of toilet paper."

Zara giggled, which was the result Luc had intended.

She was a smart little girl, sometimes scarily so. But she was way too serious for a nine-year-old. Anything she took an interest in, she pursued with the dogged determination of someone much older. She'd taken up Cajun fiddle-playing at age six, and in only three years had become proficient enough that she was going to perform at the upcoming music festival.

Loretta joined them, her arms filled with a giant basket. Luc took it from her, leaning close enough to get a whiff of her shampoo. She smelled like lavender and honey and fresh-baked bread. The combination of scents made Luc's skin tingle.

"My dad sent you some new honey samples," Loretta said, clearly oblivious to her effect on him. "Red currant— and cranberry-flavored. Those are his newest inspirations."

"I'll let you know how the guests like them."

She flashed him a shy smile. "I gave you some extra orange muffins, too, since I know you like them."

"If I didn't know better, I'd think you were flirting with me, Ms. Castille."

Loretta picked up the empty basket Luc had brought out, suddenly all business. "Same order for tomorrow?"

It was always like that. Loretta was warm and friendly until Luc tried to flirt with her. Then she shut down. Obviously she had her reasons, and Luc knew he should respect them, whatever they were. But pouring on the charm came naturally to him. It was hard to turn it off.

"Maybe some extra croissants. I've got one more guest arriving today." He always ordered a bit more than he needed. But the B and B was doing better than expected, and he liked the idea of spreading the wealth around, helping the local economy.

Loretta made a quick note on a small pad she always carried in her back pocket. "Croissants."

"You want to come in for some breakfast? There's always room for one more."

"Two more," Zara pointed out. She was a stickler for accuracy. "Can we, Mama?"

Loretta wavered. "I guess I have time for a quick cup of coffee, though we've already had breakfast. And there is something I'd like to talk to you about."

Luc's interest was piqued. He'd been wondering for a while now if there was any way to further his acquaintance with Loretta. When he'd made casual inquiries about her, he'd been told by more than one person that Loretta didn't date. Her husband had died in prison when Zara was just a baby. Granted, a tragic relationship like that was enough to put any woman off men for a while. But nine years?

Maybe if she got to know him better… Having a beautiful woman like Loretta for company would sure make his enforced stay in Indigo a lot more pleasurable.

Loretta and Zara seated themselves at the kitchen's tiny bistro table with coffee and orange juice, respectively.

"It's true what they say, you do make the best coffee in town," Loretta said after one long, appreciative sip. "It's certainly better than what they serve at the general store. That sludge is undrinkable after ten o'clock."

"What about the Blue Moon Diner? And Marjo Savoy makes a good cup of coffee."

"The Blue Moon runs a close second to this," Loretta insisted. "And Marjo's coffee is good, I'll admit that. But…"

"But you have to wait until someone dies to get a taste of it." Marjo owned the local funeral home.

Zara apparently thought Luc's observation was hilarious, because she burst into a fit of giggles until orange juice came out her nose.

"Wow, something must have tickled your funny bone," Loretta said as she wiped Zara's face with a napkin.

"I like Luc. He's funny."

"He is funny," Loretta agreed. "But his name is Mr. Carter. You know the rules."

"Sorry," Zara said, unrepentant.

"Can she call me Luc if I give her permission?" Luc asked Loretta.

"It's not really proper."

Luc, who'd been raised in Las Vegas, would never get used to the old-world manners of the South. "How about Mr. Luc?"

Loretta frowned.

"Sir Luc?"

The frown wavered.

"Lord Luc? Saint Luc?"

Finally she laughed. "Somehow I doubt 'Saint Luc' is appropriate. All right, fine, she can call you Luc." She looked at Zara. "But not in front of anyone else."

Luc took the frittata out of the oven, then checked his watch. Hell.

"I have to set the table."

"Can I help?" Zara asked. "I know where the silverware goes…Luc." As she hopped off her chair, she flashed her mother a smart-aleck smile. Loretta narrowed her eyes slightly, silently warning Zara to behave, then followed them into the dining room. Figuring she wanted to be put to work, he handed Loretta a stack of plates.

"Six settings." He got out napkins, bowls, water and juice glasses. Zara followed her mother around the table, precisely placing the heavy silver flatware beside each plate.

"These dishes are beautiful," Loretta said. "Did they come with the house?"

"Unfortunately, no. A few things were stored in the attic, but most everything of value was moved out when my grandmother's family closed down the house. *Grandmère* provided a few family heirlooms for authenticity— like the chandelier in the parlor—but I had to start new."

"You did a great job. I only vaguely recall what this place was like when I was a little girl, but the wicker and cypress furniture seems just right."

"Thanks." He'd enjoyed furnishing La Petite Maison more than he would have thought. In fact, he'd enjoyed the whole B and B experience far more than would have seemed possible a year ago. He hadn't been looking forward to two years' banishment in Indigo, away from the big-city lights he'd thrived on his whole life. But he'd have done anything to get back into the good graces of his aunt, cousins and grandmother, and to make up in some small measure for the chaos he'd deliberately created in their lives.

Fortunately, the grim, solitary life he'd anticipated had never come to pass. The townspeople had embraced him on the strength of his blood ties to the Robichaux family. He'd quickly become a part of the community, and everyone had pitched in to help with the renovation of the cabin, built by the founders of Indigo, the Valois family. They'd offered him the names of reliable workers and suppliers. They'd been eager for him to open La Petite Maison, welcoming anything that would bring tourists to town.

He wondered if they would feel the same about him if they knew the truth about his past.

"So, here's what I wanted to ask you," Loretta said, her voice shaking slightly as she placed juice glasses in front of each plate. "You know I've volunteered to coordinate the food for the music festival, right?"

Zara, her silverware duties completed, applied herself to folding the linen napkins into perfect rectangles.

"The music festival is all anyone talks about these days," Luc said. "I know what everybody's doing."

"Well…I need help. I had a committee, but Carolee went and had her baby two weeks early, and Justine Clemente sprained her ankle, which doesn't make a difference anyway because she couldn't accomplish the simplest task. Rufus's expertise is in eating, not cooking—"

Luc took the juice glass Loretta was holding before her wild gesturing caused breakage. "Loretta. Just tell me what you need. I'll do anything I can to help."

"Well, I opened my mouth and said I was going to

put on a full Cajun dinner for the musicians the night before the festival, and charge fifty dollars a head for anybody else who wants to mingle with the VIPs. But I can't find anybody to fix the food for anything like a reasonable price. We've already advertised it. Forty tickets have been sold."

"I don't know anything about Cajun food," Luc confessed, "except how to eat it."

"I know, but you have a cousin, right? Melanie Marchand, the sous-chef at the Hotel Marchand in New Orleans?"

Oh, hell. He would do anything in his power to help Loretta with her problem. But ask his cousin to cook up dinner for dozens of people for free? He'd be uncomfortable enough asking any of his family for even a small favor. A huge commitment like this was unthinkable.

"I'd love to help you, Loretta, but I can't."

Her face fell. "I'll do the asking. If you could just introduce us, I'd be forever grateful."

"I really don't think I can help." How did he explain to Loretta that his relationship with Melanie with all of his cousins—was strained at best? Although they had acknowledged him as their cousin, he no longer felt welcome in their hotel. They'd almost lost the Hotel Marchand because of him.

"Okay." Loretta flashed him a quick, false smile. "Well, it was worth asking."

"Melanie's really nice," Luc added. "Have you tried calling her?"

"I've left a couple of messages. But I wouldn't

expect her to return my call. I've contacted a dozen chefs, at least. Those who did get back to me aren't able to help. The festival is only a few weeks away. They say there's not enough time."

Zara, he noticed, was watching him closely. Was he going to be her mother's white knight, riding to the rescue, slaying dragons, producing fifty servings of gumbo, étouffée and jambalaya out of thin air?

"Let me think on it," he said, mostly because he couldn't bear to say no. "Maybe I can come up with something."

"That's all right," Loretta said quickly. "It was just a thought. I can't expect you to impose on your cousin. I'll get it done somehow, even if I have to pay through the nose. Zara, we better go. We have lots of deliveries to make." She grabbed her daughter's hand and swept out of the breakfast room, still talking.

"Thanks for the coffee and juice. I'll see you tomorrow morning. Zara, say goodbye."

"Goodbye…Mr. Carter," she said in a solemn voice, and the significance of the formal mode of address wasn't lost on him. The little minx was giving him the cold shoulder.

Mr. Carter indeed.

He'd show her. As he listened to the Volvo's chugging fade away down the road, he vowed he would come up with some way to bail Loretta out of her jam.

"Mr. Carter?" It was Mrs. Bird-watcher, poking her head into the kitchen. "We're ready for breakfast whenever you are."

"Coming right up."

He poured coffee and juice, and set out the yogurt and Loretta's delectable baked goods. Then, with a flourish, he placed the frittata in the center of the table. It was a thing of beauty.

The bird-watchers, both disturbingly birdlike in appearance, stared at the casserole with twin looks of horror.

"Is that…eggs?" Mrs. Bird-watcher asked.

"Yes, ma'am. It's a frittata."

She clamped her eyes shut. "Take it away, please."

"We don't do eggs," Mr. Bird-watcher added apologetically. "It would be like eating our little feathered friends, you see. Didn't we tell you?"

Luc guessed that meant the fried-chicken boxed lunches wouldn't go over big, either.

"MAMA, WHY DIDN'T LUC want to help us?" Zara asked as Loretta drove along the two-lane highway toward New Iberia, where she had half a dozen stops to make.

Loretta had been wondering that herself. He'd been very evasive about why he couldn't ask his cousin Melanie to help out with the music festival. She had to believe it wasn't because he didn't *want* to help.

"Probably because he didn't want to make a promise he couldn't keep. For whatever reason, he doesn't believe he can get his cousin to help us." She tried to cast a positive light on Luc's actions. Luc was one of the few people in this world Zara responded to besides her immediate family. She was unbelievably intelligent. Loretta sometimes had a hard time keeping up with her. Yet she was often shy with strangers and sometimes wouldn't talk at all for hours at a time. She'd get an expression on her face as if she were pondering some great, eternal problem, trying to work out the meaning of life.

"So what are you going to do?" Zara asked, her forehead furrowed.

"I'll figure something out. Don't you worry. This is a grown-up problem, not a kid problem. At the very worst, I'll hire one of the caterers I already talked to, and the dinner won't raise as much money for the opera house as we'd hoped." Or, more accurately, the dinner would *lose* money, and Loretta would feel obligated to fund the shortage with the money she'd been planning to use to expand her business. But that was what she got for pushing this idea in the first place before doing her research. She should have known better.

"Luc is handsome, isn't he?" Zara asked.

"That he is." Handsome, and exotically different from all the dark-haired, dark-eyed Cajuns who lived in Indigo. He had golden-blond hair and twinkling blue eyes and a smile that drove her absolutely wild. He talked differently from anyone she'd ever known, with no hint of a southern or Cajun accent. He'd obviously been raised somewhere else—out west, if Loretta's ear was any good. But he'd lived all over the world, if his casual references to France and Thailand were any indication.

Why he'd chosen to settle in Indigo, Louisiana, was a mystery and the topic of endless speculation. For all his easy charm, Luc didn't reveal much about his past except in very vague terms. The fact that he was Celeste

Robichaux's grandson ensured that he was accepted in the town. But that was about all anyone knew for sure.

Didn't it just figure that after almost eight years without a man in her life, Loretta would get the hots for some exotic out-of-towner with a mysterious past? Just like Jim. He'd been an itinerant farmer, handsome as the devil and brimming with funny stories of his exploits. To Loretta he'd been a romantic vagabond, a gypsy, and she'd embraced the notion of wandering the country, living off the land. At eighteen, she'd found Indigo a dead bore, and what better way to escape than to marry a wandering adventurer?

Living on the road with Jim had been an eye-opener for her, especially when she'd discovered how her husband supplemented his income. He stole things— food, equipment, jewelry, even a car every so often. No appeal from Loretta could convince Jim to stop committing crimes.

Then Zara had come along, and the vagabond lifestyle had lost the little appeal it still held. Loretta had wanted and needed a home.

Roots weren't for Jim. He'd been unable to hold a steady job, unable to stay at home for longer than a week at a time. Next thing Loretta knew, he'd been arrested somewhere in Texas for armed robbery. Shortly after his conviction, he'd become a crime victim himself, stabbed to death in a prison exercise yard.

Loretta had mourned him—or rather, the man she thought she'd married, the funny charmer who was never down, who was always dreaming up their next adventure. But she'd learned some valuable lessons. She no longer had a desire to see the world or be a gypsy. She'd come to appreciate the community she had here in Indigo, especially her wonderful parents, who'd never stopped loving and supporting her even when she'd made such bad decisions.

She also refused to throw in her lot with a man again, any man. Who knew what might lurk beneath the surface of even the most appealing guy? Even Luc Carter.

Especially Luc Carter.

He flirted relentlessly with her, but she suspected he flirted with every female. She didn't take it seriously, but just in case, she took care to make it clear she wasn't interested.

CHAPTER TWO

"Luc. To what do I owe this dubious pleasure?" Luc's grandmother, Celeste Robichaux, was a grande dame in every respect. She had agreed to "receive him" in the parlor of her huge Garden District home in New Orleans as if she still lived in a different era. She'd even had her maid bring them tea and French pastries.

Celeste herself was exquisitely outfitted in a linen dress, complete with stockings, pumps and a full complement of jewelry. He'd never seen her anything but fashionably dressed and perfectly pressed, whether she was attending a party or staying home to tat doilies, or whatever it was she did with her leisure time.

He'd heard horror stories about Celeste from his father. Supposedly Celeste banished him from home and cheated him out of his cut of the family fortune.

Luc had since learned there was another side to the story, and Celeste, while stern and a little bit scary, wasn't the devil incarnate. In fact, out of all his extended family, Celeste was the one who'd offered him a way to make restitution for the damage he'd done by sending him off to Indigo to renovate the summer house and start the B and B, keeping him out of jail by doing so.

"Thanks for seeing me on short notice, *Grand-mère,*" he said, adopting the French moniker his cousins used. "I have a problem and I'm hoping you'll be able to help me out."

"Is something wrong at La Petite Maison?" she asked, her nose twitching at the possibility that her now-valuable asset might be in trouble.

"No, the B and B is great. I'm making progress on the suite." He was converting one of the outbuildings to a separate suite for guests who wanted more privacy.

"Then what is it?" she asked impatiently.

As succinctly as he could, he outlined Loretta's desperate need for an experienced chef to organize the VIP dinner. Celeste listened, her mouth pursed as if she'd bitten into a bad peach.

"I fail to see how this concerns me. Why aren't you talking to Melanie?"

"I had hoped you might intercede on my behalf."

"Don't be ridiculous. I'm not your errand girl. If you want Melanie to help this Loretta person, ask her yourself."

He'd been afraid this might be Celeste's reaction. And really, there was no reason for her to care whether the music festival was a success or a flop. She didn't know Loretta. She probably didn't know most of the people involved in the festival—they were too young.

"Melanie has no reason to do me any favors."

"Oh, take off that hair shirt. I can't claim you're the most popular family member at the moment, but it's been over a year now. Everyone has mellowed. *Mon Dieu,* just ask her. Make it sound like overseeing this whatever-it-is dinner will be a feather in her cap. She'll love the chance to do something unusual."

Luc figured his doubt must have shown on his face, because his grandmother scowled at him.

"Your father certainly wasn't afraid to take risks," she chided. "That's one of the few good things I have to say about him. Surely he didn't raise a coward."

Now she was making him angry, as she no doubt intended. "Let's not bring my father into this. Anyway, he didn't raise me. He left when I was a kid and only came back a few years ago."

He stood, indicating the meeting was over. It wasn't Celeste's refusal to help him that made him angry, but the reasoning behind it. As usual, she was trying to manipulate him. Nothing gave her greater joy than playing her children and grandchildren like pawns on a chessboard in the belief that her actions were for the greater good.

But he knew better than to let his temper show. Celeste was his benefactor. If not for her, he would have no job and no place to live, and he had no idea exactly how much power she wielded with his probation officer.

He didn't want to find out.

"I'll go call on Melanie, then," he said. "Thanks for the tea."

"You didn't drink the tea," she said with a slight smile. As if she'd known he wouldn't.

CELESTE WATCHED Luc go, her smile fading. She knew her grandson thought she was a mean old lady. But she had her reasons for not interceding on his behalf.

She had to accept at least some of the blame for the events eighteen months ago that had very nearly destroyed her daughter's hotel. Luc Carter was his father's son, and his father—well, she hadn't done right by him.

For years, she'd been expecting Pierre to reenter their lives like the bad penny he'd turned into. She'd never expected it would be his son who came instead.

What Luc had done was reprehensible. But she'd seen something in him, some indication that he was not yet lost. She'd believed him when he'd claimed to have grown fond of the family he'd never known as a child. She'd believed him when he said he was deeply sorry for having tried to ruin the hotel's reputation so his disreputable partners could buy it cheap.

But she'd been worried there was too much of Luc's father in him. Thrusting the B and B on him had been her way of testing him in a situation where he couldn't do too much harm. She figured that if the hard physical labor required to renovate the place was too much, he would take off to some part of the world where U.S. authorities couldn't touch him, and that would be that.

But he'd stayed in Indigo, somewhat to her surprise, and had thrown himself into his task with great abandon, if her spy could be believed. He'd transformed a basically worthless piece of property into a showpiece and a moneymaker.

Now, she was fully committed to the idea of saving Luc Carter. It was a means of making amends for the way she'd treated Luc's father. But she needed to get the rest of the family in her corner. They wouldn't take her word for it, oh, no. Her daughter, Anne, was no

pushover, and Anne had raised four intelligent, opinion-
ated girls who, while all in favor of forgiving Luc and
welcoming him into the family, were nowhere near convinced he could be trusted.

He was going to have to prove himself personally to
them—and now, at least, he had a way to do that with
Melanie. Unless Celeste missed her guess—and she
seldom did—the motivation was a woman named
Loretta Castille.

LUC HAD NOT RETURNED to the Hotel Marchand since
that horrible night when he'd been shot and left for
dead by Richard Corbin, who'd been trying to acquire
the hotel with Luc's help. He felt a strange mix of
emotions as he gazed on the luxurious French Quarter
hotel where, for the first time, he'd felt he belonged. As
concierge, he'd been embraced by the Marchand sisters
and their mother—his cousins and aunt—even when
they had no idea he was a blood relative. They had
treated all of their staff honorably, and almost from the
beginning, Luc had begun to regret the path he'd taken
to avenge his father.

He should have listened to his gut.

But that was behind him now. He was moving
forward.

He entered the hotel lobby, and the first person he
saw was Charlotte, his eldest cousin, behind the front
desk. His mouth went dry, but he pressed ahead. He'd
e-mailed her since he'd been in Indigo, but he hadn't
seen her in almost two years.

Charlotte had spotted him, too, and there was no

welcoming expression on her face as he approached her with his best, most charming smile.

"Hello, Charlotte. Looks like the hotel is doing a brisk business today." The lobby was filled with small groups of well-heeled patrons, sipping their complimentary coffee. He could see through the windows that the courtyard outside Chez Remy, the hotel restaurant, was already filling with an early lunch crowd.

"No thanks to you," Charlotte said, but there was a hint of devilment in her eyes. He figured she must have softened since falling in love and marrying last year. "To what do I owe the pleasure?"

"Is Melanie available? Indigo is putting on a Cajun music festival in a few weeks, and a lot of fine restaurants from the area are participating. I have a special role I'd like Melanie to play, if she's willing." He'd stayed up half the night getting the wording of his request just right, so that it sounded like a terrific opportunity rather than a desperate request for charity. It was, in fact, a little of both.

"The festival's had a lot of publicity," Charlotte said. "It's been written up everywhere. End of next month, right?"

"That's right."

"Isn't it a little late to be lining up participants?"

"Yes, but the woman who's coordinating the food has run into a snafu. She asked if I would help."

Luc could see the wheels turning in Charlotte's head. A keen businesswoman, she wasn't one to let an opportunity for good public relations slip away.

"If Melanie does agree to help—and that's up to her,

of course—could the Hotel Marchand be listed as a sponsor?"

"I know we could arrange something. I can't make promises because I'm not in charge, but I'll bet Marjo—she's the organizer—would be willing to work with you."

"I'll see if Melanie has a few minutes."

Melanie offered ten minutes, and Luc didn't waste a second of it. Crowded into her office with Charlotte, Melanie and Melanie's husband, Robert LeSoeur, the head chef, he outlined how the VIP dinner had been promoted.

"I take it there are no cooking facilities on the premises?" Melanie asked. She hadn't smiled once.

"No. You would have to prepare everything elsewhere and transport it. Loretta has a kitchen and a first-class wood-burning oven you can use, and my kitchen is at your disposal, though it's very small."

Robert, who'd sat mute, arms folded, finally spoke up. "You've got your nerve, coming here and asking for favors."

Startled, Melanie placed a calming hand on Robert's arm.

"It's the nerviest thing I've ever done," Luc agreed. "None of you owes me the time of day, and I would never have come here if Loretta wasn't in such a spot."

"Who is this Loretta?" Charlotte asked.

He could have expounded for days on who Loretta was—a feisty single mom, as passionate about baking bread as some people were about a lover. A devoted daughter, helping her parents market their honey products.

A good friend, one of many who'd accepted him as an equal in Indigo. Gorgeous, bursting with energy and enthusiasm and ideas, never slowing down.

But his ten minutes were almost up.

"She owns a bakery. She's fantastic. You'll really like her."

"Luc says he might be able to swing a sponsorship for the hotel," Charlotte added.

"You're in favor of this?" Melanie asked her older sister.

"I'm in favor of anything that promotes the hotel. And…well, Luc is family."

"Yeah, the black sheep," Robert grumbled.

"Don't do it for me," Luc said. "Do it for a little town that's trying to survive. Do it to preserve your Cajun heritage. Remember, the more tourism in Indigo, the more people who stay at La Petite Maison, which is your family's legacy."

He'd played his last card. Now it was up to this impromptu tribunal to decide his fate.

LORETTA HEARD the school bus coming up the road and hurried to wrap up three loaves of cranberry bread and slap on "Indigo Bakery" stickers. When school started, she got the brilliant idea to offer free bread samples to the kids and the driver, Della Roy. Soon she'd had orders pouring in from the kids' parents—many from neighboring towns who might not otherwise have thought to try her baked goods. Today's was just a small order, but every little bit helped.

She ran outside just as the bus pulled to a stop and

Zara hopped off, though not with the usual spring in her step. Loretta handed the small bag of breads to Della. "Kane, Schubert and Cauberraux. And the shortbread cookies are for you." Della was a cookie fanatic, so Loretta baked her a few in return for delivering bread orders along with the kids. She seemed to enjoy the break in her routine.

"Thanks." Della beamed. "If you get any more business, I'm gonna be big as a house. See you tomorrow." She pulled away, leaving Zara standing forlornly by the side of the road.

It was then that Loretta noticed the bruise on Zara's cheek, and the fact her little yellow T-shirt had a torn sleeve.

"Zara, what on earth happened to you?" Loretta smoothed back her daughter's red hair, inspecting the bruise and checking for other injuries. "Are you okay?"

"Long story."

"Well, I'd like to hear it, please."

Zara headed toward the bakery, which had been built onto the front of Loretta's small frame house. The space was just large enough to accommodate a glass-front case along one wall, a commercial fridge, a marble-topped work space, and the brick oven, which dominated. There was also a sturdy oak table and four ladder-back chairs, for those times when a customer wanted to sit down with their bakery treat and consume it on the spot. An old-fashioned cash register handled the money.

Right now, though, the shop was deserted. Zara dropped her backpack on the floor with a clunk and plopped into one of the chairs.

"May I have a snack, please?"

"Of course you may." Baked goods held little appeal for Zara, since she lived and breathed them all the time. Loretta opened the fridge and pulled out a small plate with a sliced apple, some cheese and one small cookie. She poured a glass of milk and brought it to Zara, who solemnly handed Loretta a wrinkled note.

Loretta sighed. The note was from Patti Brainard, Zara's third-grade teacher.

Zara has been fighting again. Please call me. And don't worry, we'll work it all out.

Patti was a doll and Zara adored her, but Loretta was hardly reassured. Her nine-year-old daughter was getting the reputation of a thug.

"So what happened?" Loretta asked, trying not to sound accusatory.

"Thomas called me a cheater and said I was a criminal just like my daddy and I was gonna go to jail someday."

"Why did he call you a cheater?"

"Because I won his best Harry Potter card."

"Did you win it fair and square?"

"Well, I might have lost count on how many points I won on my last turn. But it was an honest mistake."

"Zara Castille, what have I told you about cheating at cards?"

"I wasn't cheating. If he'd been paying better atten-tion—"

"Never mind that. What did you do when Thomas called you a cheater?"

"I hit him with my notebook, not even very hard. And he, like, attacked me."

Loretta groaned. Her beautiful, intelligent, talented daughter was a budding juvenile delinquent.

"Before you say anything, I know I shouldn't take advantage of Thomas just because he's stupid and doesn't keep count, and I know I shouldn't hit first no matter how mad somebody makes me. But I barely tapped him."

Loretta pulled a chair close to her daughter and sat down, again smoothing Zara's bright red hair from her face. "Oh, honey, it's not how hard you hit him that's important. You've got to learn to control your temper. The older you get, the harder it is to change your habits."

"Thomas shouldn't have made fun of my daddy."

"No, that wasn't nice of him. But you're going to have to deal with not-nice people your whole life."

"I just wish—" Zara stopped herself and crammed an apple slice into her mouth. Her eyes were shiny with tears.

"What do you wish, sweet angel?"

"I wish everybody didn't know that my daddy died in prison. I wish I had a normal family."

"I wish you did, too."

"How come you don't get married again?"

"Because there's no one around here I want to marry."

"Then why don't we move?"

"Oh, sweetheart, you'd be so sad if we moved away. Your grandparents are here, and who would teach you fiddle if we moved away from Mr. Boudreaux? And even if I ever did marry again, that wouldn't erase history."

Zara sighed. "I'm sorry, Mama. I didn't mean to be bad. I'll count to ten next time, I promise."

"And you must not take advantage of little boys who aren't as smart as you. If I hear any more stories about that, I'm taking all your Harry Potter cards away."

"Mrs. Brainard already did that. She said she'd give 'em back next week."

The front door opened, and Loretta gave Zara a quick hug and a kiss before turning to greet her customer.

It was Luc, in faded jeans and a T-shirt advertising the music festival. He'd been one of the first in line to buy one, she recalled, and was selling them at the B and B. He was still tanned from putting on a new roof this past summer, his shaggy blond hair streaked with pale gold from the sun.

"Luc!" Zara jumped out of her chair, almost upsetting her milk, then halted as if she weren't quite sure what she wanted to do. Zara's reaction to Luc had been strange almost from the moment she'd laid eyes on him. At first, Loretta figured it was the fact he was blond. There weren't many fair-haired men in these parts. Zara had stared endlessly at him, despite Loretta's asking her not to because it was rude. But then she'd started talking like a magpie to him every chance she got. The only other adults Zara was that open with were her grandparents, and even they lavished so much loving attention on her that they embarrassed her into silence sometimes.

"Hi, gorgeous. Hey, what happened to you? You look

like you just got out of the ring after doing a couple of rounds with George Foreman."

"His name wasn't George, it was Thomas," Zara corrected him. Loretta's advice not to correct adults hadn't sunk in with her daughter.

"You mean you really were in a fight?" Luc sounded impressed. "I hope the other guy looks worse."

"Luc, don't encourage her," Loretta protested.

"Thomas doesn't have a scratch," Zara said.

"I used to do a little boxing," Luc said, addressing his comments to Loretta. "If Zara needs to learn how to defend herself—"

"I could have punched him," Zara insisted. "But by then Mrs. Brainard was looking and I didn't want to get in trouble."

"All right, that's enough talk about fighting," Loretta said firmly. "Luc, what can I help you with?" *Coffee cake, tea bread or me?*

"The question is, what can I help *you* with?" He had a mischievous gleam in his eye.

Loretta stifled a gasp. "You talked to Melanie?"

"I'll tell you all about it if you'll give me a sample of whatever it is I smell cooking."

"It's pumpkin bread. A new recipe." She went to the cooling rack and selected a small loaf, still warm from the oven, and brought it to the cutting board. "Talk, or you're not getting a single bite."

"Melanie said she'll do it."

Loretta's knife clattered to the cutting board. Operating on pure instinct, she launched herself at Luc, throwing her arms around his neck. "Oh, you wonderful man!"

Luc put his arms around her. "Wow, any more favors I can do for you? I like the way you say thank-you."

Oh, this felt good. Way too good. Luc was tall and hard and warm and all-male, and he smelled so...so not like everything else in her world of baking and laundry and little girls with their own special scents.

She let the moment stretch as long as she dared, then gave a nervous laugh as she extracted herself from Luc's embrace. "Sorry," she said, straightening her shirt. But it had been so long since she'd let herself get anywhere close to a man other than her father. "I'm just so excited. You've saved my skin. How did you do it? How did you convince her? What's the next step?"

"Mama, calm down," Zara said, giggling herself. "You act like Luc just handed you a million dollars or something."

Loretta hated it when Zara behaved more like the adult. "All right, then, one question at a time. What did you say to Melanie to get her to agree?"

Luc nodded toward the cutting board.

"Right." Loretta quickly cut two thick slices of the pumpkin bread and slathered them with whipped butter. She pulled out the chair opposite Zara and placed the plate of bread on the table. Luc sat, took a bite and sighed appreciatively. "Oh, man. Put some of this in my next delivery." He closed his eyes, savoring the treat, and made Loretta think of a different kind of sensual pleasure.

"I told her the hotel could have some type of sponsorship. I've already talked to Marjo and she's amenable. She's putting the Hotel Marchand logo on the banners and the program. But I also appealed to Melanie's pride, about how she'd be helping out a worthy cause and preserving her father's Cajun culture. She's actually excited about it. She wants to meet with us this week sometime to plan the menu and go over logistics."

"Us?"

"That was part of the deal. I promised Melanie I'd help. Anyway, since your entire committee self-destructed, you need another pair of hands."

She could think of all kinds of ways to put those hands to good use, and immediately felt her face heat. Why was she doing this? Why was she so intensely attracted to Luc Carter?

"When do you want to meet with her?" Loretta asked, busying herself by wrapping up the partial loaf in plastic. "Is tomorrow too soon? It'll have to be early so I can be home in time to meet Zara's bus."

"I can't tomorrow," Luc said. "I have a meeting in New Iberia. Wednesday's good, though."

"I can't on Wednesday," Loretta countered. "Back-to-back deliveries, then a doctor's appointment. Thursday?"

"I've got a big party arriving on Thursday."

"Well, shoot. I don't suppose you could rearrange Tuesday?"

"No." He didn't elaborate, and he didn't meet her gaze, either. Then she remembered Justine Clemente, the town busybody, remarking on the fact that Luc drove out of town every other Tuesday at 10:00 a.m. He'd been doing it like clockwork since he moved to Indigo.

Loretta's immediate suspicion was that he had a girl-friend. But if *she* were dating someone like Luc, she'd darn sure see him more often than every other week. Unless the woman was married…

Luc had always been a bit mysterious about his past and his personal life. Other than vague references to the fact he had hotel experience, what did she really know about him? Yes, he was Celeste Robichaux's grandson, but did that automatically make him a sterling citizen?

Well, whatever he did every other Tuesday was none of her business, and she decided not to think about it. "How about Wednesday afternoon? I can juggle the deliveries and change the doctor's appointment. My parents can keep Zara for a few hours."

"I'll see if Melanie can do it then." Luc's sunny smile returned. He polished off the pumpkin bread and the glass of milk Loretta poured for him, and all seemed right with the world again. But Loretta was determined not to forget that strange, evasive look that had come over his face.

Her husband had been a man with a mysterious past, and at first that had been part of his appeal. He'd kept so many secrets from her, all the while charming her with his flattery and his monumental plans for the two of them. When he did occasionally reveal something of himself, she felt positively blessed. And whenever she sensed his inner torture, she loved him all the more.

But the darkness inside him had been his undoing, as well as her and Zara's, for he could never be truly satisfied, not with a loving wife and beautiful daughter, not with the sweet little house her grandmother had left her, not with a decent job. He'd wanted more—more money, more control, more freedom. Uncomplicated small-town life could never have satisfied him for long.

She'd been in the process of divorcing him when he'd died, and she'd sworn that if she ever hooked up with another man—and that was a huge "if"—it would be a simple man with simple needs, someone without secrets.

Most important, any man she associated with had to be honest, forthright and without a criminal cell in his body. She was already terrified of what Jim's DNA had contributed to Zara. No way was her little girl going to be exposed to anyone who wasn't open and honest.

So Luc Carter was out of the question, no matter how much he heated her blood.

CHAPTER THREE

LUC HUMMED as he put fresh linens on the bed in the attic suite. A couple of years ago, when he'd been on the concierge staff at a luxury hotel in Thailand, he never could have imagined himself living such a quiet life in a small town, reduced to performing the duties of a chambermaid.

But he'd always enjoyed giving hotel guests the personal touch, and this was just another way of doing it. He dried the sheets outside on the line whenever possible, so they'd smell like fresh air and sunshine. He'd learned how to cook through osmosis from earlier jobs in the huge, bustling kitchens of four-star hotels, but he found he enjoyed the more intimate meals he provided the B and B guests.

He'd long ago stopped counting the months and days until his enforced restitution was completed. He still planned to take off next spring. Maybe he'd go to Greece or Italy. Jobs were plentiful for someone with his experience.

But he was in no rush to leave Indigo, which surprised him. In the past, a year or two had been about the limit of his patience for any one job, any one locale.

He sensed someone watching him and whirled around to find Doc Landry, the town's octogenarian physician, standing in the doorway. Luc smiled a welcome. "Oh, it's you."

"Boy, you're in a happy mood. I never saw anyone get so excited about hospital corners before."

"I like my work," Luc said. But that was only part of what contributed to his good mood. He and Loretta were heading to New Orleans as soon as she finished her deliveries. He would have her all to himself for several hours.

Doc was going to watch the B and B while Luc was gone. No guests were scheduled to check in today, but Luc did occasionally get walk-in business. Besides, Doc seemed to like hanging out here. He often came for neighborly visits with the guests, sitting on one of the porches with them if the weather was nice, telling them what the town was like when he was a boy.

Apparently the Landrys had been close to the Blanchards, his grandmother's family, and Doc had spent lots of time in this very house during his youth. He remembered Luc's grandmother as a young girl, and the stories he told of a laughing, headstrong teenager were a stark contrast to the stern, rigid woman Luc knew as *Grand-mère*.

Doc pitched in to help, putting pillowcases on the pillows. "Your good mood wouldn't have anything to do with the fact you're driving a certain pretty young redhead to New Orleans, would it?" he asked shrewdly.

"That doesn't hurt."

Doc's expression turned serious. "Listen, I think you should know something about Loretta."

"There are a lot of things I'd like to know about Loretta. She's a hard one to figure."

"You know she's a widow, right?"

"Yeah, I'd heard."

"Well, her husband was a piece of work. He was an itinerant farmer who turned her head when she was barely eighteen, and she married him against her parents' wishes. They traveled, lived out of their car, had a grand old time."

"Loretta? Lived out of her car?" Luc could hardly picture that. She was such a homey person. She had her bakery, her little girl. She was a sexy earth mother.

"Until she had Zara," Doc continued. "Then she wanted to settle down and become responsible. But Jim didn't."

"What happened?"

"He took off. Then he hooked up with some bad characters and got involved in a holdup. Shot someone. Got caught, went to prison."

Luc sank onto the bed, the pillowcases forgotten. "That's awful." He'd already known some of this, but the details made Loretta's situation even more disturbing. He hated to think of her as a new mother, lonely, abandoned, husband locked away. "Then what happened?"

"Her husband was murdered in prison."

The stark horror of that reality hung in the air for a few moments. "They were still married?" Luc finally asked.

"Almost divorced when it happened. It was a terrible thing. I truly believe Loretta still loved him, though she despised what he'd done, what he'd become. She grieved something awful."

"But she's over it now, right?" Luc asked hopefully. "That was several years ago." He didn't want to think of spunky Loretta as damaged. It was too sad.

"She's bounced back. Poured herself into taking care of little Zara and starting her bakery. I'm not telling you this because I like to spread idle gossip."

"Then why…" Luc got a sinking feeling in his stomach. "She would freak out if she knew the real reason I came to Indigo."

"To put it mildly. She's extremely sensitive about exposing Zara to anyone with any sort of…well, let's just say she didn't want to hire Samuel Kane to repair the roof on her house because he's had a couple of speeding tickets."

"Oh, boy."

Doc was the only person in town who knew the story of Luc's arrest and conviction, other than the chief of police, Alain Boudreaux. It was conceivable Loretta would never learn of Luc's dirty little secret. Doc wouldn't blab. But what if she did find out?

"You got a little thing for her," Doc concluded.

"A huge thing."

"She doesn't date, you know. She hasn't so much as gone out for ice cream with any man since Jim's death. She feels she's better off alone and she makes no secret of it."

"So my sordid past isn't really an issue," Luc said. "She wouldn't go out with me if I was on the Pope's top-ten list of most saintly people."

"No. Not unless you change her mind about men."

Which was exactly what Luc had intended to do. "If it becomes an issue, I'll deal with it then."

"Keeping secrets in a small town is nearly impossible, you know," Doc cautioned. "Already more than one person has speculated on where you drive off to every other Tuesday."

"You mean there are actually people in this town who have nothing better to do than keep track of their neighbors' comings and goings?"

"Absolutely. Luc, I would never tell your business to anyone else, believe me. And I happen to think maybe you'd be good for Loretta. Pretty young girl like that shouldn't be alone, and Zara needs a daddy. She's a handful, that one."

"Whoa, whoa—wait a minute. I never said anything about being a daddy. I like Zara and all, but I haven't even asked Loretta out on a date."

"Just promise me you'll be careful with Loretta's heart. I delivered her, you know. I treated her cuts and scrapes and tonsillitis and ear infections. But a broken heart I can't do anything about, and I don't think I can bear to see her in pain again. So just be careful. Be honest."

"Yes, sir. I will."

They lapsed into silence as they finished the bed linens. Luc wasn't used to anybody caring about where he'd been or what he'd done, except in the most casual way. And he'd never paid much attention to what people thought of him. If he couldn't charm his way out of a sticky situation, he would simply move on.

That sort of thinking no longer applied.

Until he'd gone to work as a concierge for the Hotel Marchand two years ago, he'd had no close personal ties. He'd called his mother every once in a while so she wouldn't worry too much about him, but that was it.

He felt different now. He didn't want to just walk away if things got uncomfortable for him. He wanted Loretta to like him and be relaxed about letting him hang out with her and Zara. He wanted to prove to his family that they hadn't wasted their compassion on him, that he was worth a second chance.

If he messed up by hurting Loretta, all the goodwill he'd been building would go right out the window.

LORETTA WASN'T a big-city person—she'd discovered that during her wanderings with Jim. She didn't like crowds, noise or smog. And on those few occasions she had to travel into New Orleans, she dreaded it.

Today had been different. For one thing, Luc was driving, so she didn't have to worry about freeway traffic or parking. He handled his SUV with skill, smoothly shifting from lane to lane. She found herself looking out the window at the city, marveling at the signs of rebuilding that were everywhere. The city was coming back after Hurricane Katrina's devastation, despite what the naysayers had predicted, proving once again how resilient the people of Louisiana were.

The meeting with Melanie Marchand and her husband, Robert, went amazingly well. Melanie wasn't anything like the snooty chef Loretta had imagined. She was friendly and funny and accessible, and she treated Loretta as if she were a new best friend. Though Loretta was just a small-town baker who worked out of her home, Melanie and Robert acted as though she were on a par with them.

Loretta had brought them some samples of her bread, and the couple had oohed and ahhed over them, swearing they were as good as anything available in the French Quarter. Melanie was brimming with ideas on how to do the dinner, and in a very short time they had a menu worked out. Melanie promised to e-mail Loretta with a list of the ingredients, utensils and volunteers she would need for the dishes that would be prepared on site. She made everything sound so easy that Loretta found herself relaxing for the first time in two weeks.

The only curious thing was the relationship between Luc and his cousins. While Luc was normally relaxed and charming with just about everybody, he was a bit stiff and formal with Melanie and his other cousin, Charlotte, who managed the hotel. They all seemed to be overly polite and wary around each other.

Loretta was dying to know what their history was. But to ask would be rude, and Luc wasn't volunteering anything.

When the meeting was finished, Luc took Loretta to the Café du Monde, where they drank strong coffee with chicory and ate beignets. Though it was October, the weather was still pleasantly warm with only the slight hint of a fall breeze. In short, it was perfect.

Loretta forced herself to stop speculating about Luc's family relationships and focused on the man himself, who had visibly relaxed the moment they were away from his cousins.

"Your beignets are better than these," Luc said.

"Don't be silly. These are the most famous beignets in the world." And she took a bite. The deep-fried pastry was pure fat and empty carbohydrates, and she loved it.

"I like yours better." He reached across the small café table, paper napkin in hand, and gently wiped at her upper lip. The gesture was very intimate—the kind of thing a lover would do. Yet Loretta felt perfectly comfortable with having him touch her that way.

"Oh, dear, have I made a mess of myself?"

"Just a little powdered sugar. Not that you don't look cute with a white mustache…"

She quickly fished a mirror out of her purse, but she saw no trace of anything on her face that shouldn't be there. What she did see surprised her: bright eyes, flushed cheeks, plump lips. She looked more alive than she had in ages. Younger, too. She saw traces of the optimistic teenager who she'd thought had died right along with Jim and all her romantic dreams.

She quickly put the mirror away. What was she thinking? She'd made the decision long ago that she would not get involved with another man. She had a full life—Zara, her parents and their honey company, her own rapidly growing business. She had no time for men, nor any inclination to adjust her life to accommodate one.

Even in the early days of her marriage, when things were still good, she'd been surprised by all the adjustments she'd had to make to please Jim. She'd grown her hair out long for him because he liked long hair, even when she thought it was a pain to take care of. When it came time to fix a meal, she knew Jim expected certain things on the table, and she had to put them there—whether she liked them or not. When she decorated and furnished their home, she couldn't go with anything too feminine.

He hadn't been unreasonable, and he had made some adjustments for her. He'd quit smoking when Zara was born, at least around the baby. Making accommodations to please your spouse was just part of marriage, her mother had explained. Any marriage, even the best.

When Jim had taken off, she'd been sad and lonely, of course, but she'd also enjoyed the freedom to do whatever she wanted, whenever she wanted. She could wear ratty old nightgowns to bed, watch weepy movies on TV, eat cheese-and-tomato sandwiches for dinner if she didn't feel like cooking.

Maybe it was selfish, but she didn't want to give up those small freedoms—not for anyone. She and Zara were doing fine on their own. And Zara—how would she react to sharing her mother with someone else? She was already headstrong. Despite Zara's vague longing for a "daddy," Loretta couldn't imagine she would welcome a new authority figure in her life.

So that was it. No men, not even Luc. But when she looked at him, her stomach swooped and her chest tightened.

"I have a couple of stops to make before we head home," Luc said after draining the last of his coffee.

"Sure, no problem."

It turned out his errands were all in the French Quarter, so they walked. He picked up some fancy scented soaps and potpourri at a funky little boutique, two cans of cherrywood stain from a woodworking shop, and a large canister of pecan pralines, which he put on his guests' pillows when he did turndown service, instead of the traditional chocolate.

His arms were full as they headed back toward his car, and Loretta grabbed one of the bags to help him out. She was having the best time, and it struck her as slightly amusing that he could discuss lavender-scented versus citrus-scented potpourri with a grandmotherly lady in a froufrou shop and not give up a single ounce of his masculinity.

Luc was as comfortable in his own skin as any man she'd ever known.

Bourbon Street was slightly crowded in the late afternoon, and they had to dodge various tourists with bulging shopping bags and the occasional party animal who was getting an early start on Happy Hour.

Loretta heard the motorbike before she saw it. She turned, and there it was, skirting around a car here, a pedestrian there, hopping up on the sidewalk when the driver couldn't get through any other way.

It was coming right at them, and Loretta was so shocked she froze in place, unsure which way to dive.

"Jeez!" Luc grabbed her and pulled them both flat against a brick wall as the motorbike whizzed past, not giving them a second look. The breeze blew up Loretta's skirt and ruffled her hair.

Several other pedestrians shouted at the maniac and

waved their fists at him, but Loretta had already forgotten the reason Luc had pulled her against him. The sounds of the raised voices receded into the background along with everything but the sensation of her breasts pressing against Luc's hard chest, his arm clenched protectively around her shoulders, their legs tangled together.

They'd have fallen over if not for the wall supporting them.

She looked up into his blue eyes, and her breath froze inside her lungs. She couldn't inhale or exhale, and she wondered if she was going to simply expire right here because she'd forgotten how to breathe.

When he bent his head down to capture her lips against his, it seemed the most natural thing in the world. The shopping bag she'd been holding slipped to the sidewalk as she met the fervent kiss with enough heat to singe her eyebrows.

Where had this come from?

He briefly lifted his head from hers to suck in an almost frantic breath, but Loretta wasn't letting him escape. Pure instinct took over as she stood on tiptoes to claim another kiss. She'd become a tigress, and she didn't care that they were on a public street.

Hey, it was New Orleans.

A nearby car honked, startling them and finally bringing them to their senses. They pulled apart at the same time, and Luc looked down at her with a sort of shell-shocked expression. She expected to see that mischievous grin of his, but it was curiously absent.

"Loretta—" he began, but his voice broke.

"Uh…" She had no idea what to say. Should she apologize for behaving like a floozy? Thank him for opening up the rusty valves inside her, allowing her to feel something deeply for the first time in years?

"Are you okay?" he finally managed.

"I think so. You?"

Gradually he loosened his grip on her. "That guy could have killed you."

The *kiss* could have killed her. She could have had a heart attack from the exhilaration. "What…" she tried again, but her poor beleaguered brain simply wasn't connecting thoughts into coherent sentences.

He leaned over to pick up the bag she'd dropped. Fortunately it was the one with the potpourri and a couple of tea towels, nothing breakable. "Shall we keep walking?"

Loretta wasn't sure her legs would hold her up. But she took one tentative step, then another, and she didn't crumple to the sidewalk.

He took her hand. The gesture was oddly innocent, given the incendiary embrace they'd just shared. Wasn't the hand-holding supposed to come before the kiss?

"That was maybe a little sudden," she said, and chanced a look at him.

Finally his grin returned. "I couldn't help it. You were right there. And I've been thinking about it all day. When you had that powdered sugar on your mouth at the French Market, all I could think about was kissing it off."

Oh, my.

"We can forget it happened if you want," he reassured her. "In fact, maybe that's the best thing. Doc told me you had no interest in dating, and I'll respect that." He paused a beat. "If I have to."

Was it true? Yesterday it had been. Today, she wasn't so sure. "Did Doc tell you why I don't date?"

"He told me how your husband died. It must have been rough."

Loretta sighed. She loved her small town, but gossip came with the territory. It would be nice if everyone didn't know her tragic history. Sometimes she wanted to sweep it under the rug, pretend it never happened. Pretend she was normal, with a woman's wants and needs.

Today, for the first time in years, she had felt almost normal. Today, the thought of getting tangled up with a man, making herself vulnerable again, didn't frighten her into shutting down.

"Even if I wanted to…to date, or whatever, I don't think I know how. The last time I went out on a date, I was in high school. Things have changed an awful lot."

"Yeah." He raised an eyebrow. "You don't have a curfew anymore."

"More than that, I'm afraid." The biggest change was four feet tall and likely to be full of questions and opinions about her mother having a male friend.

"Like what?"

"I'm just not sure how it would work. With Zara. I never envisioned myself exposing her to strange men."

"I'm not that strange."

She laughed despite the awkwardness of the situation. "Zara already likes you. She's a regular chatterbox around you, which is highly unusual. She's actually a bit shy around adults."

"Zara?"

"Really. I've always been worried that if I went out with someone, she could get attached and that would make it doubly hard on her when the relationship ends. I don't want to cause her any more difficulties than she's already facing."

"I understand. Loretta, really, it's okay. The timing's not right."

Why did he have to be so darn agreeable? If he would just argue with her a little, she might be tempted beyond her convictions. She was still warm and tingly in places that had been asleep for a long time.

They reached Luc's car just as the meter was about to expire. He put his packages in the back and unlocked her door. She climbed in, feeling horrible and sad and wishing she weren't so confused.

How often did a guy like Luc Carter come into someone's life? How many women would give up chocolate for life just to spend one night with him?

She put on her seat belt and lapsed into silence. As Luc gradually made his way out of the Quarter and onto the freeway, fighting rush-hour traffic now, he cast a worried glance at her every so often.

To her horror, her eyes filled up with tears, and the harder she tried to force them back, the worse they got, until they spilled onto her cheeks and she gave herself away with the most awful sob.

"Loretta. What's wrong?"

"N-nothing."

"Bull."

"It's just that ever since Jim went to prison, I've told myself I have to be good. I have to live my life for Zara. She's my responsibility, my legacy, and I can't mess it up. That's why I gave up men, and I've been okay with that, but now I'm not."

"Oh, God, please stop crying. I can't stand it. I'll pull over."

"No, just keep driving, I'll be fine."

"Aren't you being a little hard on yourself? Lots of single mothers don't check themselves into convents."

"I know." She found a tissue in her purse and mopped at her face. She always looked horrid when she cried. Luc probably wouldn't *want* to date her after seeing this side of her. "Just blame this on hormones or something, okay?"

"You don't have to apologize."

"I know. I'm just making everything worse."

"Would you stop it, please? You haven't done anything wrong."

"Except I'm acting like a psycho."

"A little bit," he admitted, which actually made her laugh.

"Going without sex for nine years can do that to a person." She clapped her hand over her mouth, horrified. Had she just said that out loud?

"I'm going on two years myself."

"I don't believe you."

"It's true."

"What about the girlfriend you visit every other Tuesday?" She covered her mouth again, too late to prevent those words from escaping. What was wrong with her? Didn't she have any discretion?

Luc turned to look at her, shocked. "What?"

"That's the gossip. You leave town every other Tuesday to go *somewhere*. And since you aren't dating any of the local women, the logical explanation is that you have a girlfriend in New Iberia." Loretta was ashamed to admit she was more than a little anxious to have that particular bit of gossip negated.

He didn't say anything for a long time, and Loretta desperately wished she'd kept her mouth shut. Then a slow smile spread over his face. "Busted."

"You mean you do have a girlfriend? And you kissed me?"

"It's not an exclusive arrangement."

Loretta gave an unladylike snort. She could scratch Luc off her list. Any guy who treated women like that… "Do you really have a girlfriend? Or is this your way of positively discouraging me?"

"Why would I try to discourage you when you've already discouraged yourself?" And that was the last they spoke of his mysterious Tuesday out-of-town drives.

Loretta noticed he hadn't truly answered her question.

CHAPTER FOUR

LUC MANAGED TO TURN the conversation to a less personal topic, and to his great relief Loretta said nothing more about his Tuesday outings. But it was disconcerting to realize the whole town knew about his Tuesday trips, or cared enough to guess he was seeing a girlfriend.

It was strange to think of them speculating about him at all. Though he'd lived in Indigo well over a year, he still wasn't used to small-town ways.

It was in his best interest to let them believe in the fictitious girlfriend. Better than having them find out the truth. And it was better if Loretta herself believed he was unavailable. Although he'd fought against the notion at first, he could see that Doc was right: feisty, independent Loretta had a vulnerable spot when it came to relationships. If she fell for him and then discovered the truth about him, she'd never forgive herself. And she definitely wouldn't let him near her or her daughter again.

Given his past, he wondered if that might not be for the best. What did he have to offer a woman like her, anyway? What kind of influence would he be on a child?

It was late afternoon by the time he pulled into the driveway of Loretta's parents' house, just a few blocks from the bakery. It was a warm-looking house, two stories with a big front porch. A sign in the yard advertised Indigo Honey.

"As long as I'm here," Luc said, "I should pick up some honey. I've sold quite a bit lately." Luc featured the Castilles' honey in a display near the front desk. In return, the Castilles included brochures for La Petite Maison with the orders they mailed out. It was a profitable arrangement for both of them.

"I'm sure my dad will be pleased to hear that."

Before they'd even gotten out of the car, the front door opened and a diminutive alien burst onto the porch. At least, that's what it looked like. It was about four feet tall and encased in a white jumpsuit, complete with gloves and a full-headed hood with screen netting over the face: Zara in a bee suit.

"Look at you!" said Loretta as her daughter all but tackled her in an enthusiastic hug.

Zara pulled off her hood. "Grandma cut down a big suit for me, so I could help Granddaddy with the bees. And I wasn't hardly afraid at all."

"Good for you," Loretta said.

Zara smiled up at him. "Hi, L—" She stopped herself just in time as Adele Castille walked out onto the porch. "Hello, Monsieur Carter," she said with exaggerated formality.

"*Bon après-midi,* Mademoiselle Zara," he returned.

"You speak French?" Zara asked. "Are you Cajun?"

"My dad was Creole," he said, but that wasn't where

he'd learned the French. He had a very good ear for languages and had picked up enough conversational French to get by during the few months he'd worked in New Orleans at the Hotel Marchand.

"What about your mom?" Loretta asked as they all went inside.

"Definitely *not* Creole, or Cajun." His family was one subject he didn't really want to talk about. He focused on Loretta's mother. "How are you doing, Mrs. Castille?"

"I'm very well, thank you for asking, Luc. How was your trip to New Orleans?"

"It went great," Loretta said. "Melanie Marchand is so gracious. It's going to be the most awesome dinner. Where's Papa?"

"Out fighting the webworms. Some farmer two miles away reported seeing a few, so your father's spraying every tree on our property. Those little critters can destroy a beehive in no time. Luc, would you like to stay for dinner?"

"Thanks, but I can't," he said automatically. He figured he and Loretta had seen quite enough of each other today. Not that he could ever get his fill of her, but he imagined she was ready to see the dust behind his car. "I really just came in to buy some honey. The guests love it."

Just then a door opened somewhere in the back of the house, and Zara rushed toward the sound. "Granddaddy! Monsieur Luc Carter is here to buy honey but he's not staying for dinner."

Vincent Castille entered the living room from the

kitchen, giving Luc a broad smile. He was a big bear of a man in overalls and a workshirt, with thick, dark hair slicked back from his face, and he was about as Cajun as they came.

"Well, Monsieur Luc." He vigorously shook Luc's hand. "You havin' any problems with webworms?"

"I don't think so. They're bad, huh?"

"Bad? A webworm is purely evil, not to mention being the enemy of the beekeeper. That little ol' worm gets inside the hive and you don' know it. You can' see it. The bees fly back and forth, looking busy as can be. But a few weeks later when you go to collect the honey, what happens, Zara?"

"There's no honey," she said, "only that li'l ol' worm."

"He'll talk for hours about webworms," Adele said in a loud stage whisper. "Come on, Luc, I'll get you your honey." She led him into what had once been a dining room, but was now the honey business office. Two large hutches were filled with jars of honey. Along another wall were packaging and mailing supplies, brochures and invoices. In the middle of the room was a large, well-used desk.

The Castilles blended their honey with various essences to give them unique flavors, and Luc picked out a variety until he had a dozen jars. Adele prepared his invoice, giving him a vendor's discount. He paid her, then folded the receipt and put it in his wallet. He had to keep track of every penny he spent on behalf of the B and B, or Celeste would have his head.

"What are you doing for the festival?" Adele asked.

"I'm helping with the VIP dinner. The B and B will be packed all weekend, so I'll be busy."

"No, I mean, what are you doing to promote La Petite Maison? We're renting a booth with Loretta in the food section. We're going to pass out free samples and sell honey and baked goods. They're expecting thousands of people to come through Indigo over the weekend. It's an unparalleled chance for promotion."

"I hadn't really thought about it." He'd just been glad for the extra business during the festival itself.

"You could share our booth," Adele said, because that's the kind of person she was. "In fact, we were thinking of getting two, because one isn't that big. You could have extra brochures printed up, and give away ten-percent discount coupons. Or advertise your bayou cocktail cruises," she added.

"My what?" Luc didn't even own a boat, except for a pirogue, which he'd let the bird-watchers borrow.

"Lots of B and Bs do extra stuff like that as an additional revenue stream. Cruises, ghost tours, walking tours of the town."

Luc was still pretty new at this entrepreneur stuff, but he had to admit, Adele had a point. She was the genius behind Indigo Honey's success.

But he didn't think he was up to sharing a crowded booth with Loretta for an entire weekend. He had enough trouble keeping his hands off her as it was. If she wasn't interested in hooking up with him, he would respect her wishes. But that didn't mean he wanted to torture himself by deliberately putting himself in her path.

"I don't think so," he said. "It sounds like a great idea, but I'm going to be really busy that weekend with guests."

"Well, if you'd like us to set out some brochures, just let me know." Adele seemed unruffled by his refusal, but Loretta looked troubled.

"You're sure you won't stay for dinner?" she asked as she walked him back to the car. "About the kiss and all…I overreacted. It was just a kiss." Her face turned a becoming shade of pink.

Luc liked to think it wasn't "just a kiss," but a way-above-average, special, mind-blowing kiss. It had been for him, anyway. "I have to get back. Doc's keeping an eye on the place, and I'm sure he'd like to get on home."

"All right, then. Thanks for driving and…and, well, everything."

He reached out and brushed his knuckle across her cheek, and she didn't shy away from his touch. In fact, her changeable hazel eyes turned darker, and he saw hunger in them. "Don't worry so much."

"I'll try not to." The words came out barely a whisper.

LORETTA KNEW she'd done the right thing. But then why did it feel so awful? She had more on her plate right now than she could possible deal with. Maybe Luc was right and she *was* entitled to a social life, single mom or no. But not now, and not with a man who kept so many secrets.

When her mother found her a few minutes later, she

was still standing in the driveway, staring after Luc's car, lost in thought.

"Loretta?"

She snapped to awareness. "Oh. Guess I was day-dreaming."

Adele put an arm around her daughter's shoulders. "About Luc?" she asked hopefully. Adele would have been more than happy to see Loretta settled down with a nice son-in-law and a few more grandkids.

"No," Loretta said quickly, then laughed at herself. "Okay, yes, I was thinking about Luc. What do you suppose it is about me that craves something *different?* Why was Jim so alluring when the local boys left me bored to tears? Why does the mysterious man from out of town have such appeal?"

"Lord, Loretta, you can't compare Luc to Jim. They're like two different species. Luc is responsible, stable. A businessman. There's nothing wrong with Luc."

"Except that I don't know anything about him. And he has a girlfriend."

"He's Celeste Robichaux's— He has a girlfriend? Who?"

"Someone out of town. He says they're not commit-ted. He was all mysterious about her. I don't need that. I don't want mystery or intrigue or adventure. I don't want a man, period. I have enough to keep me busy."

Adele chuckled. "Sometimes what we want and what we get are two different things. He's awfully handsome. And he's very good with Zara. Not every man gets on with children, you know."

"Mama! Don't encourage me. I've only just made up my mind to leave it be, and you're weakening my resolve."

"I'm just saying, is all."

WHEN LUC GOT BACK to the B and B, he found Doc on the veranda with his guests, two elderly sisters from Baton Rouge. They were all drinking mint juleps and seemed to be getting along very well.

"Luc," said Isabel, the older sister. Or maybe it was Ernestine. He got the two mixed up. "You didn't tell us about the complimentary cocktails on the veranda. What a delightful surprise!"

How did he tell Isabel, or Ernestine, that the mint juleps were as much a surprise to him as to the guests?

"And such delightful company," said Ernestine, simpering a bit. "Are you and the doctor related?"

"Uh, no."

"But I knew his grandmother quite well," Doc said with obvious fondness. "She and I used to sit on this very veranda when we were hardly more than teenagers, and sip mint juleps just like these."

"Those were different times," said Isabel dreamily. "When men were gentlemen."

"Speaking of being a gentleman…" Doc pushed up from his rocking chair. "Excuse me, ladies." He motioned for Luc to follow him inside. They entered the parlor, but neither of them sat down. Doc gave Luc a hard stare. "How was your day?"

Luc sighed. "You were right. Loretta doesn't need a man in her life, and I'm not sure she'd let one in, anyway."

"What happened?"

"I did exactly what you told me not to do. And it was a mistake." Luc paused. "I made her cry."

"Why? How? Damn it, Luc—"

"Chill out, I didn't do anything wrong. I just stirred up some feelings she wasn't ready to deal with." He set the box of honey on the table. "Don't worry, I've learned my lesson. From now on it's strictly hands off. Not that I don't wish it could be otherwise."

LUC TRIED TO RECONCILE himself with that decision. He tried hard. But there was no way to avoid Loretta when she delivered baked goods to his home every morning and talked to him at least twice a day regarding the VIP dinner, which would be staged at the town's almost 200-year-old opera house.

She kept their conversations businesslike—overly so, in fact—and he got the idea she was every bit as uncomfortable as he was. But she was bound and determined to make the dinner a success and raise money for the opera house renovation, so talking with him was a necessity.

When the phone rang just after lunch on a Wednesday the week after their trip to New Orleans, Luc fully expected it to be Loretta, and he braced himself for his reaction. Just the sound of her voice did provocative things to him these days.

"La Petite Maison," he said into the phone.

"Luc. What are you doing to promote the bed and breakfast at the Cajun music festival?"

"*Grand-mère.* How nice to hear from you." And how

typical of her not to start the conversation with any pleasantries. She never minced words, his grandmother.

"I just heard they're expecting thousands of people at the festival. People who will drive all that way to hear a bunch of fiddle-playing would also be interested in our bed-and-breakfast. The Hotel Marchand is an official sponsor now. I don't want La Petite Maison to be left out."

"I was planning on having plenty of brochures printed up—"

"Not good enough. We must have a presence. Our B and B is one of the most visible, profitable businesses in Indigo."

"Ooookay." Actually, some of the ideas Adele Castille had mentioned were swimming around in Luc's brain. He was always looking for ways to give his customers added value, so they would want to come back— and tell all their friends. "We can sponsor historic walking tours of Indigo. This town is packed with history." The tragically romantic story behind the opera house was a doozy. "I can recruit some of the local teenagers to be guides."

"Go on," Celeste said, indicating neither approval nor disapproval.

"We can advertise our bayou cocktail cruises."

Long silence. "When did we institute cocktail cruises?"

"We haven't yet. We need a boat."

"Mmm-hmm. What else?"

"Loretta, the woman who provides our baked goods, will have a booth," he continued reluctantly. "She's offered to share her space with me. She's giving away free samples of her breads, which would be great advertising for the B and B."

"How much does this booth cost?"

He named the very modest price.

"Get two. Or three. I want you to proceed with these ideas, Luc. Both Robichaux and Blanchard used to be important names in Indigo. We can't simply let others lead the way. Do what you must, within reason, to ensure La Petite Maison is visible. I'll send you some things you can use to decorate your booth. You can make it like a little museum. And look around for a boat. We used to have one when I was a girl, and all the young people would pile in for moonlight rides…." She halted the dreamy memory abruptly. "I want a progress report in a week's time." Not waiting for Luc to agree, she hung up.

"Oh, boy," Luc muttered. As if he didn't have enough to do helping out with the VIP dinner, he had shop for a boat, print up more advertising brochures—and turn an ordinary festival booth into a museum.

Celeste didn't ask for much.

His first order of business was to call Loretta, a task he couldn't help but look forward to. He took the cordless phone to the laundry room. Sheets and towels were in constant need of attention, and Luc had gotten into the habit of throwing in a load when he was on the phone. He dialed Loretta's number from memory. Not that he'd had occasion to call her often, but he'd unwittingly memorized everything about Loretta. He even knew the license plate on her car.

"Indigo Bakery."

"Loretta." He loved saying her name, and he couldn't help that he spoke it like a lover.

"Yes, Luc. What can I do for you?" Her voice was decidedly cool. He tried not to take it personally. She was no doubt deliberately distancing herself from him, just as he'd done with her. His news might not be all that welcome, after all.

"If the offer to share a booth at the festival still stands, I'd like to take you up on it."

"Oh. Oh, sure, that'd be great," she said, but Luc got the distinct impression she'd changed her mind. "I'm worried we might be a bit crowded, though. Three businesses, one booth."

"That's the good news. My grandmother has agreed to spring for three booths. We'll have plenty of room." He wasn't sure if Celeste had intended for him to share the booths, but he'd pretend to have misunderstood.

"Wow. That's very generous of her."

"There's a catch. We have to make this triple-sized booth highly visible and very fancy. Like a museum, Celeste said. She'll pay for everything, but I was hoping you and your mom would have ideas for making it eye-catching." And he outlined his plans for the bayou cruise, which had been Adele's idea.

"But you don't have a boat."

"Celeste said to buy one."

"Wow. This could be really cool. Hey, I know, you could have a raffle. Give away a free weekend for two. Get people to sign up, and you've got an awesome mailing list."

"You could do the same—have a raffle for a big gift basket with bread and honey—"

"You're right. Oh, but when will I ever have time to do all this? With the dinner—you wouldn't believe what has to be done to the opera house just to meet code requirements. I'm going nuts already."

"Don't worry, we'll work on it together." Damn, he liked the sound of that way more than he should have. And what about his promise to Doc that he would leave Loretta alone? But how could he leave her alone when they would be working long hours side by side?

Hell, Doc would just have to understand. Celeste had spoken, and he knew as well as anyone that you couldn't say no to Celeste.

"If you say so. We'll need to get together and start making plans and shopping lists and— Oh, my God. Oh, my God!"

"What?" Luc demanded. She sounded downright panicked.

"There's black smoke pouring out of my brick oven. The fire's gone out of control!" And she hung up.

CHAPTER FIVE

LUC DIDN'T THINK, he acted. He dialed the head of the volunteer fire department, Chuck Bell, to tell him there was a fire at the Indigo Bakery. Then he ran out of the house, jumped into his car and headed to Loretta's as fast as he could go. He narrowly managed to avoid hitting a fat chicken that had wandered out onto the road in front of Yvonne Valois's house.

He was reassured when he caught sight of the Indigo Bakery and didn't see any flames. But the front door was open, and wisps of black smoke wafted out.

He was out of the Tahoe before it came to a full stop and ran full tilt for the bakery entrance. "Loretta! Loretta, where are you?"

She appeared at the door, waving a newspaper to dispel the smoke, and she was coughing.

Luc reached in and grabbed her arm, dragging her out into the fresh air. "The fire department is on its way."

She shook her head. "There's no need. The fire is out. The chimney on my wood stove wasn't drafting, that's all."

"Did you forget to open the flue?"

"No, I'm sure it was open."

Luc called Chuck back and let him know he could call off the brigade, everything was fine. Then he went inside to assess the situation. The smoke was already dissipating.

"I don't think there's any real damage," Loretta said. "Thanks for coming so quickly."

Luc walked through the bakery back into Loretta's house, though she hadn't invited him to do so, and found a back door off the kitchen. He opened it to help draft the smoke. On the way, he couldn't help take notice of Loretta's home. It was clean and uncluttered, decorated simply, but the walls were painted in vibrant shades—turquoise, bright green, magenta.

It seemed there was a wild side to Loretta Castille that Luc had yet to experience. But he wanted to. Oh, yeah.

He found an empty box by the back door. Flattened, it made a good fan, and he joined Loretta back in the bakery to get rid of the last of the smoke. The scent was still in the air, and probably would be for a while, but at least his eyes were no longer burning and Loretta had stopped coughing.

"Have you ever had trouble with the oven before?" he asked.

"No, never. My father drew up the plans—after consulting fifteen books on the subject, of course—and we built it together. I have a small commercial oven in my kitchen, but I liked the idea of using a wood stove. Bread just tastes better, somehow. I've been experimenting with artisanal bread—I really want to push it at the festival."

"What's artisanal bread?"

"It's bread crafted by hand the old-fashioned way. Traditionally, you use just flour, water, salt and yeast. You knead it by hand and make it into round loaves, the way bakers have done for centuries—you don't use pans."

"I see." Though he wasn't sure he did. He was all in favor of natural ingredients, but he wasn't sure what difference a wood oven or the absence of a pan would make. Still, Loretta was the expert.

"It's all the rage in California. I want to print up a little flyer about how it's made. But I need to experiment more so I get it just right. And I can't do that if my oven won't draft!"

Luc walked over to the oven and inspected it. He hadn't paid that much attention to it before. But now that he knew Loretta had helped to build it, brick by brick, it was a lot more interesting. There was a large lower compartment, where the wood was stored, and a smaller baking chamber above, which was currently covered with white residue from a fire extinguisher.

"How does it work?" he asked.

She was more than happy to explain. "You build up the fire in the baking chamber. And when it gets good and hot, you push the embers to the edges and put your bread right on the floor of the oven. The oven stays hot for hours and hours, so you just keep baking."

"Can you make pizza in here?"

Loretta laughed. "You're such a guy. Yes, pizza made in a wood-burning oven is to die for." She joined him, standing close enough that he could smell the lavender scent of her shampoo even underneath the smoke. "Ugh, what a mess." She poked at the soggy wood, which was now covered with white powder. "This fire extinguisher stuff is bound to be horribly toxic, and it's all over my beautiful oven."

"I'll help you clean it up."

"You don't have to do that."

"Just let me, okay?"

She smiled. "All right."

Using insulated gloves, Loretta removed the ruined logs from the oven, and Luc carried them out to the backyard, where he doused them with the hose to be sure they were truly extinguished. When he returned, Loretta was scouring the inside of her oven with soapy water and a scrub brush. He found another brush and went to work on the oven's exterior and the floor, all of which had gotten sprayed by the fire extinguisher.

When everything was sparkling clean and cool to the touch, Loretta dried it with old towels.

"The damper is definitely open," she said. "I need to look up inside the chimney and see if it's stopped up or something. Maybe some leaves collected in there."

"You're going to climb inside your oven?"

"It's not hot. I'd barely lit the fire when it started smoking and I put it out right away."

She got a flashlight and pulled a chair over to the oven and climbed onto it, then leaned back and stuck her head in the baking chamber so she was facing up. Then she wiggled her way farther inside. Luc watched with fascination.

She switched on the flashlight. "I can't see anything.

It's pitch-black and I should be seeing blue sky. There's definitely something stopping up the chimney."

"Maybe we should go at it from outside."

She emerged from the oven and climbed off the chair, allowing Luc to give her a hand for support.

"Maybe I should call my dad."

"No need to bother him," Luc said. "We can figure this out."

"Are you willing to get up on the roof?"

"Sure." In renovating the cottage, he'd gotten used to being up on the roof. "Where's your ladder?"

She showed him where the ladder was stored, and he leaned it against the roof and climbed up while she watched anxiously. "I could call a chimney sweep."

"I can handle it," he said again with more confidence than he felt. He'd never unclogged a chimney before. But how hard could it be?

The roof pitch wasn't too steep. Luc made his way to the chimney and peered down.

Something hissed at him.

He jumped back. "Holy—"

"What?" Loretta called.

"There's a creature in there."

"A creature?" She sounded alarmed. "What kind of creature?"

"Toss me up the flashlight."

She did, and when he shone it down the chimney, he saw two beady black eyes in a masked face. "Raccoon. And it's not very happy. I think it's stuck."

"Oh, the poor thing! I almost burned it up. Can you get it out?"

Only a complete fool would stick his bare hands inside a chimney with an angry raccoon. They grew big in bayou country. "Can you get me those gloves you used earlier?" They were thick, heat-resistant gloves, similar to the kind firefighters used.

She disappeared inside and returned moments later with the gloves, tossing them up to him. They were a tight fit, but he hoped they would offer some protection if the creature decided to bite.

"Now, maybe if you could push it from below, I could pull it from up here," he said.

"You're kidding."

"Unless you want to take your chimney apart brick by brick—"

"No! I'll—I'll get a plunger and try to push with that. At least I won't hurt it that way."

Luc liked the way Loretta was worried about the welfare of an animal most people considered a pest. While he waited for her to find a plunger and stick it up the chimney, he looked back down at the raccoon, who was making a low growling noise. This was not a friendly animal. Maybe he should call the fire department and have them deal with this. It wasn't a cat stuck in a tree, but close enough.

"All right," Loretta called from below, her voice barely carrying through the obstructed chimney. "I'm ready."

Sending up a silent prayer that he wouldn't end up with rabies simply because he wanted to be Loretta's white knight, Luc reached down the chimney. Sure enough, the first thing the raccoon did was bite him. But his teeth couldn't penetrate the Kevlar-and-leather glove. Luc grabbed the thing by the scruff of its neck and pulled, but it wouldn't budge.

"Are you pushing?" he called.

"I'm pushing!"

The raccoon came loose like a cork out of a bottle. It freed itself from Luc's grip, climbed up his arm, over his head and down his back, clawing and hissing and basically scaring the bejeezus out of Luc before breaking free and running wildly for the nearest tree branch.

Luc's arms windmilled as he tried to regain his balance, but it was hopeless. He fell backward and rolled off the roof, landing with a thunk on the ground.

The fall knocked the wind out of him, but he didn't think he'd broken anything. He lay there, trying to suck air into his lungs as Loretta came crashing out the back door with the plunger still in her hands.

"Luc! What happened? What was that noise?" She looked up at the roof, expecting to see him, and when she didn't, she glanced all around, finally spotting him lying on the grass.

Her face crumpled into an expression of horror. "Luc!" She was at his side in an instant. "Are you hurt? What am I saying? You fell off the roof. Of course you're hurt."

He opened his mouth to reassure her, but he still wasn't breathing normally, and all that came out was a croak.

She cupped his face in her hands. "Don't try to move. I'll call Doc Landry. He'll know what to do." She started to get up, but he grasped her hand before she could escape.

"I'm…okay. Just had…the wind…knocked out of me. Give me…a minute."

"Are you sure?"

He liked having her worry over him. He liked it a lot, so much that he considered milking this accident for all it was worth. But no, he couldn't do that. That was the old Luc, the one who wasn't above manipulating people for his own selfish interests. He'd made a solemn vow not to live like that anymore, to be honest—well, as honest as he could be—with everyone he dealt with.

So he forced himself to push up onto his elbows, then his hands. "I'm fine, Loretta. I'll have a few bruises and I'll probably be stiff and sore, but that's all."

"If you're sure…"

"I'm sure. I'm just thankful you have a one-story house."

Still, she helped him to his feet and brushed the leaves and grass off his shirt.

"Oh, you're bleeding." She indicated a place on his arm where the raccoon's claws had dug in during its panicked escape. He probably had a few more claw marks on his head. "Did the raccoon do that?"

"Uh-huh."

"Where is it?" She looked around warily.

"Halfway to Mississippi by now. That was one terrified animal."

"Well, it's no wonder, after I almost lit its tail on fire. Come on inside. I'll patch you up and fix you lunch. It's the least I can do for you after you nearly killed yourself."

"Don't you have bread to bake?"

"I always have bread to bake."

Loretta made him take off his shirt so she could treat a grazed area on his back, where he must have scraped against the rain gutter on his way over the edge of the roof.

As she dabbed antibiotic cream all over his body, the minor pain ebbed and a pleasant tingling took its place. Oh, yeah, he could get used to this. It had been a long time since anyone had cared this much about his welfare, and it felt damn nice.

Nice enough to make him want to rethink the rolling-stone lifestyle he'd enjoyed for most of his adult life.

As she ministered to a nasty gouge near the small of his back, her hand lingered, and Luc tensed. He knew exactly what had snagged her attention—a small, round, slightly puckered scar that could only be one thing. If she asked about it, he would have to tell her the truth. Lying about having a girlfriend had been bad enough.

But she said nothing, and after a moment she continued her first aid.

Relaxing slightly, Luc entertained Loretta by describing his close encounter with nature, playing it up for laughs until she had tears streaming down her face. "It's not really that funny," she insisted. "You could have been killed. Next time anything like this comes up, I'm calling in a professional, I don't care how much it costs."

LORETTA HAD known Luc was handsome, that he had a good build, but she'd had no idea until she'd seen him shirtless what a gorgeous specimen he truly was. All the hard work he'd done renovating the cottage had given him a hard set of muscles and a golden tan. When he stretched forward so she could put a bandage on his scraped back, she saw a narrow strip of paler flesh peeking out from his jeans, which made her wonder if he wore underwear.

What did they call it when you went without? Going commando?

Her face heated, and she chastised herself for letting her thoughts wander in that direction. She was taking advantage of Luc's injury to run her hands all over his smooth, muscled back, forgetting that he belonged to another woman.

"There, I think that should do it," she said briskly. "You can put your shirt back on." She'd done everything but run her fingers through the light dusting of gold hair that grew in a diamond shape between his nipples.

Argh! She was doing it again.

"Let me just get the fire started again, and I'll find something for lunch."

He put his shirt back on, much to her disappointment. "You don't have to feed me—"

"No, I insist." She wasn't quite ready to let him escape. It was so novel, having a man in her home. It had been just her and Zara for so long.

She found she was nervous as Luc watched her start the fire, using straw and matches and small, dried branches.

"Wouldn't it be easier to soak the logs with lighter fluid?" he asked.

"Oh, heavens, no. This is artisanal bread, remember. I have to do things the way they did hundreds of years ago. I don't want any of that chemical residue in my oven."

She was pleased when the fire caught right away. It had taken her a long time to learn the proper technique.

"How about grilled cheese sandwiches and tomato soup for lunch? It's not very fancy, but I always crave it when the weather starts to turn cool." It wasn't exactly sweater weather yet, but at least the hot, muggy days were giving way to pleasantly cool weather, and a few of the leaves had started to turn. They didn't get much in the way of fall foliage in Indigo, but their autumn had its own charms.

"That sounds great. What can I do to help?"

She appreciated that Luc wasn't like most men she knew, incompetent in the kitchen. Well, that wasn't completely true. A lot of the Cajun men knew how to cook up a mess of crawdads or barbecue a hunk of meat. But Luc actually cooked a full breakfast for his B and B guests on an almost daily basis, and he sometimes provided lunch or dinner, too.

"Where did you learn to cook?" she asked. "Did your mother teach you?"

Luc hadn't been very forthcoming about his past, usually tossing off flip answers when she asked him anything to do with his family. But she guessed after the raccoon incident, his guard was down, because this time he answered her honestly.

"My mother couldn't cook at all. She worked in a casino—long, long hours—and she always ate free at work. I had to fend for myself, and I decided if I didn't want to live on peanut butter sandwiches, I'd better learn my way around a stove."

"So you're self-taught?"

"No, not entirely. I've worked in hotels all my life, sometimes in the kitchen. I learned a lot by watching some really good chefs."

"Hmm, maybe it's in your blood, what with your cousin Melanie being a chef, too. Was it your mother or your father who was a Robichaux? Oh, that's a silly question," she said before he could answer. "Since your last name is Carter, it must be your mother."

"No, actually, my father was Celeste Robichaux's son. My mother's name was Carter. She took it back and changed mine, too, after she divorced."

"Oh." *Way to put your foot in your mouth, Loretta.* "I'm sorry. I shouldn't have assumed—"

"Don't worry about it. I didn't know my father well growing up, and that's probably a good thing. He was the proverbial black sheep of the family, although it took me a long time…"

"What?" She paused in slicing the cheddar cheese to look at him, wanting him to continue. She was surprised at how badly she wanted to know more about him.

He abruptly clammed up. "Sorry. You don't want to hear all that old family history. People who drone on and on about their past are a dead bore. And if you're going to all the trouble to fix me lunch, you don't deserve to be bored."

"I wasn't bored," she said pointedly, but she sensed

that was all she was going to get right now, so she didn't press.

She thought, not for the first time, that there was something very mysterious about Luc and the way he'd shown up in Indigo. Something painful had brought him here. Maybe it was a divorce, or a broken romance, or that mysterious long-distance girlfriend. Maybe he'd lost a job and hadn't had any place to go, although Loretta doubted that. With his startling good looks, his charm, his intelligence and his experience, this man would have no trouble getting a job anywhere he pleased.

She was dying to know, but she sensed she wouldn't get the answers she wanted from him, not till he was ready to reveal them.

CHAPTER SIX

LUC AND LORETTA talked of trivialities while they ate their lunch, and afterward she expected Luc to leave. So she was surprised when he asked if he could watch her make her artisanal bread.

"It's not that interesting," she said, though she was thrilled at the idea that he wanted to hang around some more.

"It is to me." His voice was low, seductive. Or was that just her, misinterpreting everything? "Besides," he added, "someday I might be stranded in the wilderness with only some flour and a couple of matches. I might need to know how to do this."

She laughed at his justification. He wasn't trying to seduce her. He was just Luc being Luc. And the attraction she felt toward him wasn't simply because he was an exotic outsider. He was an interesting person. And, most flattering, she supposed, he found *her* interesting.

"Fine," she said, "you can help me."

Preparing the dough was a simple enough process. Loretta sifted equal amounts of white and whole wheat flour, then some sourdough starter and just enough water to form a thick dough. She floured her marble preparation surface and began to knead.

Luc leaned against the counter and watched intently. "Where did you get your starter?"

"Believe it or not, I inherited it. I come by my baking genes honestly—my Grandma O'Donnell baked all the time and I spent my formative years helping in her kitchen."

"So you're part Irish. I wondered where you and Zara got all that red hair."

She didn't confess that she hadn't always been a redhead. Her natural color was a rather dull brown. Zara's beautiful red hair had inspired Loretta to try to match it, and the short spiky cut meant she didn't have to spend a lot of time caring for it.

Her red, spiky 'do also ensured she stood out in a town full of dark-headed Cajuns. There was something inside her that refused to be ordinary or commonplace. It was the very thing that had gotten her into loads of trouble as a child and had caused her to rebel and marry Jim against her parents' wishes.

It was the thing that made her start this crazy baking business in a small town in the middle of nowhere, where conditions weren't that favorable to a small retail business. She wanted to make a mark, *be* someone special.

And it was the thing that drew her to Luc. Because he was special, and the fact he was attracted to her made her special, too.

The logic was flawed, she was sure of it. She should be setting a good example for Zara by living a sane, ordered, responsible life. Lord knew Zara had much of her mother in her, which was both good and bad. Certainly Loretta would prefer her rebellious streak to Jim's penchant for criminal behavior.

"You can help knead," she said to Luc. She could use another pair of hands. She'd made a big batch of dough, which required kneading in two parcels, anyway.

They stood side by side at the counter working the dough. Loretta had always enjoyed kneading bread. It put her into a meditative state. She felt connected to the earth and all its bounty with the heady smell of flour and yeast all around her.

But now the experience contained a whole new level of sensuality. She found herself paying attention to Luc's strong hands working the springy dough, squishing it between his fingers, then balling it up and pounding it with his fists. Her mouth went dry and other parts of her sprang to life as she imagined those hands on her, kneading, massaging…

She took in a sharp breath and forced her attention back to her own ball of dough. But she couldn't block out his presence when he was standing inches from her and she could smell him and hear his breathing and the rustle of his clothes and see his sinewy forearms as his muscles stretched and bunched.

"How long do we do this?" he asked.

"Hands getting tired?"

"No. It feels good. I like the feel of the dough."

Oh, Lord. Luc was a sensualist, like her.

"I guess that's good enough. Now we let it rise." She got out a couple of bowls and set the balls of dough inside, covering each with a clean towel. She set them near enough to the oven that they would receive some ambient warmth.

"How long do they have to rise?"

"An hour should do it."

"So what do we do while we're waiting?"

Did she only imagine the blatant invitation in his voice? What happened to their agreement to ignore their mutual attraction?

It wasn't really an agreement, she realized. She'd been the one to declare she didn't want or need a man in her life. Luc had never said he wouldn't try to change her mind.

"I have a jillion things to do—like package up orders for the school bus." She explained about how she marketed her products to the parents of the kids on Zara's bus.

"Very clever," he commented. "You get the kids hooked on free samples, then they beg their parents to buy sweets from you."

"Mostly it's the parents who get hooked. But, yeah, that's exactly the idea. Free samples are the way to go."

She was pleased she had turned the conversation to something as innocuous as marketing, skillfully ignoring the challenge in Luc's eyes. Now, she should just thank Luc again for all he'd done and send him on his way. Didn't he have a B and B to run?

But she couldn't find the words to send him away. She simply liked having him around. It would be way too easy to get used to this.

She went to her bakery cases, where she'd stored the items she'd baked that morning in her conventional oven. Thank goodness they hadn't still been on the cooling rack during the raccoon incident. They'd have gotten all tainted with smoke and she would have had to start over.

Luc came up behind her, close but not touching. She could feel his body heat through his clothing and hers. "I could help you with that. Then you could get it done in half the time."

"Luc, you don't have to—" She stopped. Luc was nibbling the back of her neck. He'd moved his hands to her waist, where he now held her gently but insistently, preventing her escape—as if she'd wanted to escape.

"If you got your work done in half the time," he said in that low, sexy voice of his, "you'd have time for…other things."

"Luc!" His name came out a squeak, rather than the forceful admonition she'd intended. "What if someone walked in and found you…and me…"

"You haven't had a customer since I got here."

Yeah, more's the pity. "But you said…we said…the other day…"

"I'm sorry, I can't help myself. I never knew baking could be so sexy."

She couldn't really criticize him for that thought, since she'd had the same one. Would it hurt? Would it really hurt? She was a woman with a normal woman's needs. They were both single and unencumbered…except for Luc's girlfriend.

He moved his hands to her abdomen and pulled her closer, and she leaned back against his hard chest.

"Luc, I…your girlfriend."

"Mmm." He stopped. Good, he ought to feel guilty.

He swiveled her around so he could look into her eyes. His face was so close she could see each individual eyelash. "Is that all that's bothering you?" he asked.

The girlfriend made for a handy excuse. "Is that all? I don't know how you were raised, but I happen to believe in loyalty and faithfulness and honesty. My husband had none of those qualities, and it was very hurtful."

"I'm sorry he hurt you." Luc caressed her face. She could have stopped him, could have sidestepped him and insisted he put some distance between them. But she didn't. She was weak. "The last thing I want to do is hurt you."

"I'm not talking about me. I'm talking about *her.*"

He had the gall to laugh. "Loretta, there is no her. There is no girlfriend."

"But you said—"

"I figured it would be easier for us both if you thought I was committed elsewhere, that's all. I shouldn't have lied about it, though, and I won't anymore. My life might not be an open book, but I won't lie again."

Strangely, though she had no reason to, she believed him.

She also realized he'd neatly eliminated all her stated reasons for resisting him. And when he was looking at her like that, with fire in his eyes, she was helpless to resist, anyway. He could have a hundred girlfriends, and she'd be applying for the position of Girlfriend #101.

He was waiting for her to say the word.

She knew what the sensible answer was. But she

didn't feel like a sensible woman. The fire building inside her right now was hotter than the one in her oven, and it was burning all the sanity right out of her. A few inches, that was all that separated their mouths—all that separated Loretta from crossing a threshold that would change her life forever. After making love with Luc Carter, she would never be the same, of that she was sure.

The voice inside her that made her do crazy things—the one that was usually subdued by life's responsibilities and practicalities—suddenly was yelling into a megaphone. *Take the risk! Life is meant to be lived.*

She took a step forward, closed the gap, and kissed him in a way that would leave no doubt as to what her answer was.

"Loretta," he whispered between kisses, and her name spoken in his husky voice was a turn-on in itself.

But they couldn't stay here in the bakery. "Just a minute." She pulled out of his embrace long enough to flip over the sign on the door to Closed and engage the lock. When she turned back, Luc was standing right behind her, apparently unwilling to let her get far out of reach.

"I'm not running away," she said.

"I wouldn't let you."

LUC STILL COULDN'T believe he'd done this. He'd promised Doc and himself that he would leave her alone. He knew she was fragile, yet he was powerless to resist her.

She returned to him and took his hand, leading him

into her house, to her bedroom. Holding her hand gave him an oddly sweet feeling, especially given that explosive kiss they'd just shared. He shouldn't be feeling sweet. He should be feeling turned on, and he was.

But he also felt a strange tenderness for Loretta that wasn't the norm for him.

He'd never gotten emotionally entangled with a woman. He'd had his share of girlfriends, but he'd always been careful not to pick the sweet ones, the vulnerable ones who might get hurt. He wasn't the sticking-around type of guy, and every girlfriend he'd ever had knew that going in.

Loretta didn't, not really.

He should tell her. She had a right to know. But as they entered her bedroom, with its pink walls and frilly bedspread and every girlie item he could imagine, he knew the time for explanations had passed.

"I'm a little rusty." She cast her eyes down in a self-conscious way that had Luc's heart doing flip-flops.

"Me, too," he admitted. Now that he thought about it, this was probably the longest he'd gone without sex since he'd lost his virginity to a Jamaican hotel maid at age sixteen. Lately he'd had other things on his mind. "But I don't think I've forgotten how." He pulled her close again and kissed her, more tenderly this time. He didn't want her to be scared.

She sure didn't kiss as if she were scared—or out of practice. After a few seconds of soft kisses and nibbles, Loretta heated up like a roman candle. She locked her mouth onto his and pressed her body against him until he was the one who thought he was going to burn up.

She still smelled slightly of smoke, which only enhanced the image he had in his brain of the two of them going up in flames.

He slid his hands under her gauzy blouse, using the tips of his thumbs to graze the undersides of her breasts. Her bra felt all silky and lacy, and he was surprised that he didn't have the urge to dispense with it and get on with the good stuff.

Because it was all good stuff. Every sigh, every breath against his skin, the way her spiky hair felt against his cheek. The ends were stiff from whatever product she used to make it stand out, but when he burrowed his fingers into the hair close to her scalp, it was soft as the finest silk.

He pulled her shirt over her head and stopped to just look at her. One great thing about sex in the afternoon was the natural light pouring into the bedroom.

When he stared for too long, she blushed. He'd already forgotten he was trying to make her comfortable, so he pulled her against him again and just held her. "Do you have any idea how gorgeous you are?"

"Don't be silly," she said. "I'm average in every way."

Average? Surely she didn't actually believe that. "No, babe. I've seen average and I've seen stunning, and I know what camp you're in."

She laughed. "You've been with lots of women."

"Does that bother you?"

"No. A man who can have any woman but chooses me, well, at least for this moment—that feels good."

This moment, and a lot of others if he had his way.

He wished now he hadn't told Doc he'd keep away from Loretta. He'd meant to, but he wasn't that strong. "You know what else feels good?"

"I bet I can guess."

"Naked skin against naked skin, that's what." He pulled his own shirt off, and then they were racing to see who could get their clothes off first. Shoes got kicked under the bed, underwear went flying, and they came together again, breathless. Luc pressed his arousal into the cradle of her hips and marveled at how well they fit together.

They still hadn't touched the bed, but Luc kept looking at it. They stood near it, exploring each other with fingertips and mouths and tongues. Loretta was surprisingly fearless in her explorations, as if she wanted to experience him with all of her senses.

He could spend a lifetime discovering all there was to know about Loretta Castille.

She surprised him again by boldly grasping his arousal.

"Whoa, careful there." He laughed a bit nervously. She had no idea how precariously he was balanced, or how easy it would be to send him over the edge. A couple of years of celibacy had given him a hair trigger, and he didn't want this to end quickly.

"Should we…you know, get into bed now?" she asked.

He found her combination of bold action and timid words endearing. So many intriguing contrasts. He pulled the covers back on her poofy four-poster bed, and a light, flowery scent drifted up.

The woman perfumed her sheets. She couldn't have known he'd be here today, so she must do it on a regular basis, just for herself.

"It's a very feminine bed." She sounded embarrassed. "You'll probably feel silly lying in it."

"The only thing I feel is turned on. But for the record, I love your bed and I'm honored you're inviting me into it." He sat on the edge and pulled her down into his lap, prolonging his sweet torture as her bottom pressed against him.

In one deft move he leaned back and rolled them both onto the bed. The mattress was softer than anything he'd ever slept on. "You have a feather bed."

"Just a feather mattress topper. What can I say? I'm self-indulgent."

"I'm planning to indulge you."

LUC'S WORDS SENT tendrils of pleasure along Loretta's nerve endings. She could hardly believe she was doing this, and she felt like she was doing everything wrong—responding hotly at the wrong moments, talking when she should shut up, thinking of her own pleasure instead of Luc's.

But she was at the mercy of those damnable hormones. She could blame them for the misfiring neurons in her brain, too, that caused this temporary lapse in judgment. Her will had simply disappeared, and all she could do was go along for the ride, and a highly enjoyable ride it was.

Luc nudged her onto her back, and at first she felt pure relief that he was going to put an end to the suspense. Her blood was churning, her skin hot, her breath coming in short spurts. She was ready to see this through, ready to know what it was like to make love with Luc.

But he had other ideas.

He started by kissing her again, very thoroughly, his tongue darting in and out of her mouth in a teasing way. She made a noise low in her throat, a sound of need that was, again, embarrassing but over which she had no control. She'd hoped he would take it as encouragement that she was ready, that he wasn't rushing her.

But he was the one who wouldn't be rushed, she realized, as his attention wandered to her neck, which he kissed and nuzzled. Meanwhile his hands weren't idle. He explored her breasts as if they contained the great mysteries of the universe.

She squirmed under his touch. She was afraid she was simply going to implode from all the stimulation. Then he took her nipple into his mouth and sucked gently, and a cord seemed to stretch inside her body, straight from her breast to her core.

To her total amazement and embarrassment, she did implode. He wasn't even touching her…there. She was one great big uncontrollable ball of female need and he was taking full advantage. All she could do was gasp with the overwhelming pleasure of it all.

He chuckled low in his throat, and she cuffed him lightly on the ear. "You think that's funny?"

"Not funny, exactly," he said, looking up at her with a wicked smile. "But very enjoyable."

"In case you were worried, you haven't lost your touch." But she silently added that she was pretty sure she hadn't lost hers, either. It was like riding a bicycle, right? She reached between their bodies and found his rigid erection, and his smile abruptly disappeared.

"Oh, honey." He rolled over onto his back. "What are your plans?"

"Wouldn't you like to know?" And she pleasured him the way she knew men most loved to be pleasured, hoping he would exhibit the same lack of control that she'd shown.

But he had more discipline than she did—or maybe she *had* lost her touch. Because although he obviously enjoyed what she was doing, he didn't climax right away.

After a short while, Loretta found she was feeling all squirmy again. Giving him pleasure had turned her on again. Abruptly she straightened to her knees, and at Luc's questioning look, she swung one leg over him and prepared to take what she wanted.

"Oh, now, wait a minute—"

"I don't want to wait."

He smiled at her audacity. "When you're riding a bicycle for the first time in years, you don't immediately start doing wheelies."

"I like wheelies." She grasped the iron-hard length of him and guided him to her. She was hot and slick with need, and he stopped pretending to want anything else.

She started to sheathe him, slowly at first, but then she just needed to fill herself with him.

"I can't…control things as well…from this position." Luc's face had gone rigid, his eyes closed.

"That's the idea. I want to see you lose control." And she started to move.

"You'll get your wish." He grasped her by the hips in a vain attempt to slow her down. But now she was off and there was no stopping her. She slid up and down the length of him, drawing him in more deeply each time, wondering if she'd developed a whole new set of nerve endings, because she couldn't remember sex feeling anything like this before. She closed her eyes and gave in to it, and to her amazement, she came again with a burst of heat so explosive she actually looked down at herself to see if she was still in one piece.

She caught Luc's grin of triumph just before his face tensed and he grimaced. "Oh. Lo, you…I…" But whatever he'd been trying to say got caught in his throat as he found his own pleasure, thrusting violently inside her two or three times, his hands gripping her even more tightly. She would have bruises where he held her—bruises where his fingers clutched.

Something to remember this crazy afternoon by…for a few days, anyway.

As her own climax faded, she slumped against him. He wrapped his arms around her and she savored the closeness, the feel of his sweat-slicked skin those last few precious seconds they were joined, before his body relaxed completely and she pulled away from him.

"Loretta." The way he said her name was almost a growl.

"Luc."

"Are you by any chance on the pill?"

CHAPTER SEVEN

TALK ABOUT COMING BACK to earth in a hurry.

"Uh, no," Loretta said.

"Ah. Then I guess we should have had this conversation a few minutes ago."

"You know, it never occurred to me. Which is pretty stupid."

"Hell, it's not as if I don't know better." He sighed. "I've never in my life forgotten that little detail."

"And I've never in my life *had* to think about it. Jim and I never used anything, and it took me two years to get pregnant. So we probably don't have anything to worry about."

"Still."

"You're already sorry, aren't you?"

He kissed her on the nose. "Oh, hell, no, I'm not sorry. I shouldn't have even brought it up. Let's not borrow trouble. I just want to lie here with you."

"It was good, huh?" She was embarrassed that she needed the validation, but she felt pretty inept at the moment.

"Good doesn't even get off the starting blocks. I've never...let's just say you tested my powers of control beyond any reasonable limits. I almost came when you took off your bra, and it just got better from there."

She appreciated his frank appraisal of their love-making. But something niggled at the back of her mind, something she needed to worry about—besides the fact she'd just had unprotected sex with a man who she was pretty sure had no burning desire for children. She looked out the window, noticing the angle of the sun, and it hit her.

She looked at her watch.

"Oh, my God. Omigod! Get up, get up, get up!" She leaped out of bed as if the sheets were on fire—and they almost had been, she reflected.

"Loretta. What—"

"Zara's bus will be here any minute!"

Thank God he caught on without her having to explain. He scrambled quickly and yanked on clothes. This mad dash was not the way she would have wished to end her interlude with Luc, but it couldn't be helped. She was not prepared to explain to Zara why Luc was lounging around in her bed with no clothes.

Loretta pulled the covers up over the bed while Luc replaced the ruffly throw pillows their passion had dislodged. She spritzed a bit of perfume around the room, though Zara didn't normally come into Loretta's room until evening, when they cuddled in the big bed to read together.

Then Loretta dashed into the master bath to freshen up as best she could. She almost cried when she saw herself in the mirror. She did not look like a responsible mother/businesswoman. She looked like a wanton slut.

She fluffed up her hair, put on a smear of lip gloss—despite her panic, her vanity hadn't completely deserted her—then emerged to find Luc fully dressed, leaning one shoulder against the door frame with his arms folded, watching her with a trace of amusement.

"You *do* think I'm funny," she accused him.

He straightened, walked up to her and kissed her soundly. "I told you, I just enjoy everything about you. I suspected there might be a very passionate, sensual woman beneath that homey little bread-baker you present to the world, and I was right."

They returned to the bakery, and Loretta reversed the Closed sign to Open just as the bus pulled up at the corner and Zara hopped off. She looked around curiously, probably wondering why her mother wasn't there with her schoolmates' bread orders, then shrugged and headed for the house, dragging her heavy backpack.

"I'll call you later," Luc said. She could tell he wanted to kiss her again, but he resisted. She wanted to tell him that he didn't *have* to call, that she'd gone to bed with him without any expectations or promises. But truth be told, she wasn't quite that modern. She wanted there to be something between them.

How scary was that?

"We need to talk about the Cajun dinner," she said, then wanted to curse herself. Now he would think she was trying to eradicate what they'd done.

He grinned. "Of course we do." And he pushed his way out the door just as Zara was about to enter. She stopped short, surprised. Then a huge smile spread across her face. "Hi, Luc! Are you leaving?"

Luc gave Zara's pigtail a gentle pull. "I have to run, gorgeous. Next time I visit, maybe you can play your fiddle for me."

"I'm not good enough yet!" she objected, though Loretta knew otherwise. The piece Zara planned to play at the festival was coming along nicely. She was a fast learner and practiced with the dedication and intensity of a true artist.

"When you're ready, then." And he was gone.

Loretta realized she was staring after Luc's car, lost in thought, when Zara tugged on her shirt. "Mama. Can I have a snack?"

"Of course you may, sweetheart. How was school?"

"Good. I got a hundred on my spelling and Mrs. Brainard let me feed Mr. Chuzzlewit." Mr. Chuzzlewit was the class mascot, a large, lop-eared rabbit.

"Excellent."

"Mama, where are your shoes?"

Loretta looked down, surprised to see her bare toes peeking out from the hem of her jeans. "Oh. I guess I took them off a while ago and forgot to put them back on."

"Better not let that health inspector see you barefoot in here."

"I'll go put my shoes on right now." Goodness, she really was rattled. While Zara fixed her own snack, Loretta disappeared back into the house, pausing in her bedroom to hug herself. She shouldn't feel so happy. She'd made a stupid decision to make love with Luc. They weren't even dating. And to completely forget about birth control…

But even that couldn't dull her feelings of elation. Sometimes a girl just had to do something crazy that was totally, completely for herself, and damn the consequences.

She hunted for her shoes and socks, finally locating a sock hooked on one of the bedposts. My, she *had* been in a hurry to get undressed. She grinned as she pulled it down and sat on the edge of the bed to put it on.

"Mama?"

Loretta jumped a foot. Zara stood in the doorway. "Yes, sweetheart?"

"I can't find the peanut butter, and why was Luc here?"

"Oh, rats, we're out of peanut butter. I meant to get to the store today, but things got so crazy. That's why Luc was here. I had a little fire in my oven because the chimney was stopped up. And you'll never believe what was up there." She told Zara the story as they returned to the bakery and scrounged up some crackers, cream cheese and a persimmon for a snack.

Zara laughed at the picture her mother painted of the frantic raccoon climbing over Luc to make its escape and Luc falling off the roof.

But then she turned serious. "Why didn't you call Granddaddy?"

"I was already on the phone with Luc when all the black smoke came pouring out of the oven. He jumped in his car and raced over here to help."

"That was nice of him."

"Luc is a very good man. We're lucky he chose to

move to Indigo." She sneaked a cracker off Zara's plate and nibbled on it, then decided to make herself a real snack. She was starving. She supposed hot sex could burn up a few calories.

"Mama?" Zara said. She sounded as if she were in a question-asking mood, and Loretta had to be prepared for anything. Last week, she'd asked Loretta to explain what an STD was.

"What is it, sweetheart?"

"I think you and Luc should get married."

"Oh, do you now?" Loretta tried to sound casual, but her heart was pounding in her ears. Had Zara seen something, sensed something? Did she know?

"My friends all think you're a lesbian."

"What? Zara, do you even know what a lesbian is?"

"Yes, Mother," she said in that impatient way she adopted whenever Loretta underestimated her intelligence. "It's a lady who likes other ladies instead of men. And, let's face it, Mama, you don't even go out on dates with men."

Great. Her nine-year-old daughter was giving her relationship counseling. "Zara, for the record, I do like men. But who has time to date? Besides, we have it pretty good, don't we? Just us girls?" Zara had given her the perfect opportunity to introduce the idea of Loretta having a relationship with a man. In fact, she was encouraging it. But the idea terrified Loretta.

She was used to her lifestyle. Comfortable. Although it sure hadn't taken very much encouragement on Luc's part to get her thinking about making some pretty big changes.

"It's just that I want…" She sighed. "Oh, never mind."

"Is this about having a dad?" Again?

Zara's eyes filled with tears. "I want a dad. The Girl Explorers are planning a father-daughter hike and cookout, and I'm the only one who doesn't have a dad. Katie Zelleger said she would share her dad with me, but it's not the same."

Loretta's heart went out to her little girl. She had no idea what it felt like to grow up without a father, because her own parents had been so loving, so supportive and always there for her.

"I bet your grandfather would go with you," Loretta said brightly.

Zara gave a halfhearted smile. "Yeah, I'll ask him. But a real dad would be better. And Luc would be a good dad. And you like him, and he likes you. I can tell these things."

So wise. Loretta could just imagine what Zara would be like as a teenager. She would know *everything*—or at least, she would believe she did.

"I know it's tough sometimes, being without a dad. But I can't just go marrying a guy because it would make our lives more convenient."

"But you could hook up with him."

Oh, Lord, where did she pick up these phrases? "You mean date him?"

"Date, hang out, you know. Kiki Madison doesn't have a dad, but her mom has a boyfriend and he's really cool. He takes her to the movies sometimes, just her and him. That's almost like having a dad."

Loretta felt as if her heart were getting kicked repeatedly by a mule. She'd had no idea Zara was harboring these longings for a father figure, or that she felt isolated because she didn't have a dad. She'd thought Zara coped beautifully with the sad facts of her biological father. She seemed like such a strong little girl. But appearances could be deceiving.

Such as all Zara's friends thinking Loretta preferred women. Was that the impression she gave people? That she was some sort of man-hater, or antisocial?

It was tempting to tell Zara that yes, she would hang out with Luc. Luc seemed to be hinting that he wanted some kind of relationship with her. That would make Zara happy, at least for a while.

But Zara's fantasies would only build from there. She would start seeing Luc as a father figure and hang her hopes for a happy family on him. And when it didn't work out, she would be crushed.

"Luc is a good man," Loretta said again. "And he likes you very much. But I'm not sure how he'd feel knowing we're talking about him as husband and father material. He might be the kind of man who shies away from settling down."

"You mean like my real dad," Zara said dejectedly.

"Well, yeah."

Suddenly Zara brightened. "Want me to ask him?"

Loretta gasped. "No, honey, I don't think that would be a good idea. Please try to understand. Just because Luc is nice and we like each other doesn't mean we would be compatible…hooking up."

"But you could try," Zara said in small voice.

"I don't think that's going to happen," Loretta made herself say. A few minutes ago, she'd been tempted to dip her toe into that murky relationship pool. But she couldn't let Zara get her hopes up when there was so little chance of anything working out in the long term. "But Granddaddy is a pretty darn good substitute. He was a great dad to me when I was growing up. I bet he would be thrilled to go on that Girl Explorer hike with you."

Zara brightened slightly. "Yeah, he's fun. Remember when I took him to show-and-tell and he brought honeycomb for the whole class?"

"He did that for me when I was your age, too." Sometimes Loretta forgot to be grateful for her parents. But Zara was right. A grandfather was fun, but it wasn't the same as a real dad.

"So, YOU BROKE your promise."

Luc and Doc were sitting on one of the B and B's upper verandas. The cabin had four porches, perfect for sitting in the evening to catch a cool breeze or watch the sunset.

One of the things Luc had learned since moving to Indigo was how to relax and live in the moment. Before, he'd always been living on the edge—dreaming and scheming about his next move, never satisfied with where he was.

But here in this peaceful place, looking out across an expanse of lawn still green despite autumn's arrival, and the slow-moving Bayou Teche, it was hard not to relax.

Luc had confessed to Doc what had happened

between himself and Loretta. He needed advice. The woman had turned him inside out.

Doc tamped down his pipe and lit it, but he didn't take a draw. Instead, he just enjoyed a quick whiff of the aromatic smoke before it fizzled and went out. He'd quit smoking years ago, but he still liked everything that went with smoking—the feel of the pipe, the smell of the tobacco, the way a match flared to life.

"I confess, I'm not a strong man. She had her hands all over me, doctoring my scrapes, and it just…went from there. She didn't exactly have to be coaxed."

"I guess I saw this one coming, despite my warnings," Doc said, shaking his head. "My question now is, what do you plan to do about it?"

"I don't want to just pretend it didn't happen, that's for sure." But apparently Loretta did. She'd been coolly professional in her attitude to him the last couple of mornings as she'd delivered his orders of baked goods, and she hadn't included any bonus muffins just for him, as she had before. She'd made sure Zara was with her so Luc couldn't talk about anything personal. And she'd been screening her calls.

"Doc, you were all worried I would use Loretta and then toss her aside. But did you ever expect her to do that to me?"

Doc gasped with mock indignation. "How dare she? Now your reputation will be ruined."

"I'm serious. She won't give me the time of day."

Doc sobered when he realized Luc was truly pained by the mess he'd created with Loretta. "Playing hard to get, maybe?"

"I don't think so. I think maybe she regrets what we did and wants to forget about it. And I don't."

"Maybe she's dumping you before you have the chance to dump her. Some gals don't want to be the one left behind."

"I had no intention of dumping her."

"Well, what *are* your intentions?"

Luc had been thinking about what he wanted between Loretta and him ever since they'd made love. But he was no closer to an answer. "I want to be with her. For as long as it lasts."

Doc shook his head. "That won't work with her."

"So I'm supposed to ask her to marry me? Why is it that guys are supposed to know exactly what they want from the very beginning of a relationship? Don't we get a chance to try things on for size?"

Doc chuckled at that. "A try-it-before-you-buy-it, break-in period. A money-back guarantee."

"No! You're being deliberately obtuse. I'm not crazy here. I don't want to take advantage of Loretta, I want to date her."

"And sleep with her."

"That's generally what happens when men and women date, yeah. Maybe in your day, you'd take a girl for a buggy ride and you'd be engaged, but it's a little different now."

Doc laughed again. "We had cars. I'm not that old. But actually, we took girls for boat rides. Nothing like seeing an alligator to get a girl in a romantic mood. Did I hear you were looking for a boat?"

How did Doc know that? "I found one in St. Martinville. A sweet little pontoon boat with a canopy. *Grand-mère* already okayed it." Was that how he knew? Celeste?

His grandmother also had an uncanny way of knowing everything Luc was up to. Were Celeste and Doc sharing information? Interesting.

They didn't talk anymore about Loretta. Luc figured Doc had no more idea what to do about her than he did. But Doc hadn't told him to keep away from her, which Luc saw as an encouraging sign. Maybe he thought Luc was worthy of Loretta after all.

Not that Doc's approval helped Luc a whole helluva lot. He was just going to have to catch Loretta alone and pin her down. Pin her down to that feather bed of hers and make love to her until she saw reason.

CHAPTER EIGHT

LORETTA WAS ASHAMED of herself, truly she was. She knew she wasn't handling this thing with Luc well at all. In fact, she was acting like a first-class bitch. But when it came to questions of her child's welfare, everything else took a backseat, including her love life.

She simply couldn't have Zara building elaborate fairy-tale fantasies about weddings and daddies starring Loretta and Luc. But she hadn't figured out how in the world to explain this to the man in question. He would think she was crazy to even bring up the subject of marriage when they'd never been out on a date.

But better crazy than just plain mean, which was how she felt now. The few times she'd seen Luc since they made love, she'd clammed up completely for fear Zara would misinterpret friendliness for…well, for something else. Yesterday, she'd seen the pain and confusion in Luc's face and she'd realized she had no choice. She had to talk to him.

Which was why today she'd dropped Zara off at school early, made all of her deliveries, then driven to Luc's—alone. He hadn't placed an order for today. He probably didn't have any guests, which was sometimes the case during the week. Or maybe he just didn't want to see her.

She was relieved to find his Tahoe parked in the carport. She pulled up behind it and got out, carrying a basket with some special treats just for him. She felt like Little Red Riding Hood, off to visit the Big Bad Wolf. Not that Luc, with his laid-back charm, was a wolf. But she sensed a hidden intensity beneath the surface, and it both drew her and frightened her.

She knocked on the kitchen door, and when no one answered, walked right in, which was what people in Indigo did.

"Luc?"

"Be down in a minute," he called from upstairs. "Help yourself to coffee."

Luc's coffee, which always smelled so good, was a temptation, but Luc himself was a stronger lure. Loretta followed his voice up the wide cypress stairs. She found him in the hallway on a ladder, changing a light-bulb.

"It's just me," she said, not wanting to startle him.

He glanced around the vintage globe. "Oh. Hi." He took a whiff. "Those wouldn't be cranberry-orange muffins, would they?"

"They might be. And pumpkin bread. And some toffee-crunch coffee cake."

He pulled a rag from the back pocket of his faded jeans and shined up the globe before climbing down. "Is this to make up for the rest of the week? Three deliveries, not a single free sample."

"That wasn't on purpose. I was so busy this week I

didn't have time to bake extras. But this *is* a peace offering."

He gave her about half a grin, which nonetheless sent her stomach swooping. How did he do that?

"They'll go better with coffee."

They went back downstairs and Luc poured them each a mug. She took a sip of the rich brew, as if it were a shot of whiskey for courage. "I've handled things badly."

"You won't get any argument from me." Luc looked out the window, obviously feeling as uncomfortable as she did. "If it was a mistake, just tell me. But don't make me guess. I keep wondering what I did wrong."

"Oh, Luc, you did everything just right, believe me."

"Is this going to be one of those, 'It's me, not you' speeches?"

"Well, it's definitely not you. But it's not exactly me, either."

"Who does that leave?" But before she could explain, he got it. "Oh. Zara."

"Yeah."

"She…doesn't approve of me?" Luc was only half joking.

"No, just the opposite. She thinks you're perfect daddy material."

If Loretta hadn't been so miserable, the look of panic on Luc's face would have made her laugh. "She said that? You didn't tell her…I mean, she doesn't know what—"

"I didn't say a word. But children can figure out more than we give them credit for sometimes. She senses something between us. But I had no idea she'd spun it into an elaborate fantasy."

"What did you tell her?"

"I told her she was out of line, that there was no chance."

LUC KNEW HE SHOULD HAVE felt nothing but relief that Loretta understood him so well. He was crazy about her and Zara both, but he wasn't family-man material. He never stayed in one place, for one thing. He changed jobs a lot, usually because he got tired of the same place and the same people all the time, and his income was erratic—he could be rolling in money one month and counting his pennies the next.

Although his mother loved him, she'd been gone a lot, working long hours to pay the bills and, later, going to school so she could get a better job. She'd also gone through a series of men after his father left, pinning her hopes on each one, then feeling crushed when they didn't meet her expectations. Luc simply hadn't been born with the constancy gene that made a good husband or father.

But, as perverse as it was, the fact that Loretta had dismissed the possibility so quickly irked him. Was he that bad of a catch? He used to get two or three marriage proposals a year. Okay, they were mostly women wanting a green-card marriage, but still.

"I don't know if I did the right thing," Loretta said, "but I can't have her getting her hopes up only to have them dashed. I had no idea she felt the absence of a father so keenly. She doesn't remember Jim at all."

"She wants *me* to fill the father role?" The notion seemed very strange to him. He'd been on friendly terms with children before, but he'd never had one take a liking to him the way Zara had.

"You've been good to her. You don't condescend to her. Most adults treat her like a baby, and she's quite aware of that."

"I don't know how to treat her any differently."

"And I wouldn't want you to," Loretta hastened to say. "But under the circumstances, maybe it's best if we quit while we're ahead. I don't regret that we made love. It was wonderful. You made me feel beautiful and desirable in a way I haven't felt since before Zara was born. But I don't think it's meant to be."

Her words had the sound of a well-rehearsed speech. And he didn't like it, not at all, even though he knew Loretta was right. They had no future, and she wouldn't want him, anyway if she knew he was on probation for a felony. Besides, he wouldn't be staying in Indigo much past the first of next year…. Still, he didn't like what Loretta was saying one bit.

"Zara's a smart girl," Luc said against his better judgment. "We could explain things to her."

"And tell her what, exactly? That we're having a temporary fling?" She shook her head vehemently. "That's not the sort of example I want to set for my daughter. How can I expect her to understand that she should avoid casual sex when she sees her mother embracing it?"

Luc wanted to object to the words "fling" and "casual." What they shared sure didn't feel like that to him.

"How about we tell her we just don't know where it's going, but we want to find out? We like and respect each other, we want to spend time together…."

"When there's no chance of it working out in the long term?"

Was that true? Was there absolutely no chance?

"I plan to live in Indigo the rest of my life," she said. "I got my rolling-stone urges out of my system a long time ago. This is my home, Zara's home. The bayou country is in my blood. You'll be moving along, and don't even try to deny it."

He sighed. She'd made her case, damn it. The mere thought of tying himself down to one place made him feel uncomfortable. It was true he'd felt no particular urge to leave Indigo, even after more than a year, which surprised him. But how much longer would that last?

Luc drained the last of his coffee. "Living in the moment isn't always a bad thing."

"I know that. And there was a time I did live in the moment. When Jim and I first married, we lived out of our car, moving across the country picking produce for grocery money. I sure didn't think about the future then. We had a lot of fun, and I don't regret it. Not all of it, anyway."

Luc had a hard time picturing Loretta as a drifter. She was so deeply rooted in Indigo now.

"But there's a time for being responsible, and for me, that time started when Zara was born. Maybe when she's grown I can be a little crazy, but not now."

"So we just go back to the way we were? Feeling the pull and doing nothing about it?"

"I don't see any alternative."

Luc knew he couldn't go back. Now that he knew what Loretta's skin felt like, what she smelled like, the little noises she made in the heat of passion, he couldn't go back. Memories of their lovemaking would haunt him every time he saw her.

Or even when she was nowhere near.

"If you want to, you can find someone else to provide your baked goods—"

"Don't be ridiculous. You're asking me to give up your delectable body, but don't make me swear off cranberry-orange muffins, too. Have mercy."

Finally she cracked a smile. "Thank you for not hating me."

"I could never hate you, Loretta. I saw what hate and bitterness did to my father, and I won't do that to myself. My motto is forgive and move on. Though I guess technically you haven't done anything wrong, except let me talk you into bed."

Her smile faded. "You won't tempt me again, will you?"

"Would it work?"

She sighed. "Probably."

But he wouldn't feel good about it. "I'll be on my best behavior when I'm around you. Fair warning, though. My best behavior isn't exactly stellar."

She pushed back her chair. "I really have to go. I have a zillion things to do for the festival."

The music festival. Luc had agreed to share a combined booth with Loretta and her family, and he'd promised Celeste he would make their display look like a museum. The only step he'd taken so far was to buy the boat so he could advertise the bayou cruises. "We also need to decide how we want to do our booth."

She gasped. "I forgot completely. I've been so busy dealing with everyone else's booths—"

"I can work it out with your parents. You have enough to worry about."

She extracted a bulging Filofax from her purse and pored over the calendar. "I can't just dump it on y'all. Can we meet on Sunday?"

Luc had a packed house over the weekend, but he agreed, anyway. "You sure you don't need any help before then?"

She stood decisively. "You've done so much already. Getting Melanie to agree to do the dinner has been a huge coup. I can handle the rest."

He stood, too. "Thanks for the goodies. You're going to make me fat."

"Hmph. Not likely."

They shook hands, which seemed ridiculously formal after all they'd shared. But the gesture served to seal their agreement, so it was the right thing to do. She left quickly, without looking back, and Luc watched her beat-up station wagon depart down the long drive, his heart heavy.

LUC HAD UNEXPECTED walk-in guests arrive that afternoon, so he called and left Loretta a message to bring a few goodies the following morning. The sound of her voice on the taped greeting gave his heart a brief lift, but then his mood plummeted.

He didn't like the way things had turned out. In the past, if a relationship with a woman went south, he simply moved on to the next one. But of course, here in Indigo there wasn't exactly a crowd of eligible, good-looking women looking to warm up the sheets with him.

Not that there weren't some pretty ones. Joan Bateman, a best-selling mystery author who'd made her home in Indigo, was attractive in a mature sort of way. He'd noticed her when he'd first moved here. But she was older than him, and, anyway, she'd recently become engaged to her literary agent. Then there was Sophie Clarkson, who'd come to Indigo a few months ago to settle the affairs of her godmother. Luc had felt a kinship with the woman almost instantly, since she was from the city and something of an outsider, like him. But she'd had a teenage romance years ago with Indigo's Chief of Police, Alain Boudreaux, and they were now married and expecting their first child.

And Marjo Savoy, who ran the local funeral parlor, was downright beautiful, but he'd had no interest in any of the local women after meeting Loretta. And now that she had eliminated any possibility of an affair…he still wasn't interested.

Thinking about Loretta, he realized that for the first time since he had opened La Petite Maison, she was late. Fortunately he hadn't eaten all of the goodies she'd brought the day before, and they were still fresh, so his guests were well supplied. But as the morning wore on and Loretta didn't show, he became worried.

He knew it wasn't his place to check on her. He had

no right to feel protective or proprietary toward Loretta. But he did.

When he returned from taking his guests for a boat ride on the Bayou Teche, where they were fortunate enough to see a six-foot alligator sunning on the shore, neither Loretta nor her baked goods had arrived.

He called her.

She answered her phone, breathless, and when he said his name, there was a long silence before she finally spoke. "I can't believe I completely forgot to deliver your order."

"Don't worry about it, I managed," he said, relieved she wasn't lying in a ditch somewhere. "I was concerned about you."

"I am so sorry. You just cannot believe how crazy my day has been. I've been inundated with calls from restaurants all over the state wanting to sell food at the music festival. Marjo told me not to turn anyone down who's legitimate, but we're outgrowing our space. The people who are building the booths want to charge extra for overtime, the health inspector is on my case about permits and inspections—" She halted abruptly. "I'm so sorry. I shouldn't be dumping this on you. Your next order is on the house, okay?"

"That's not necessary."

"Still."

Luc wanted to prolong the conversation, but he could tell she was in a hurry, so he said goodbye. But it wasn't like Loretta to forget a delivery. He hoped she wasn't in over her head with the festival. Being in the hotel business, he had some experience with special-events planning, and he knew how quickly preparations could spin out of control.

Loretta showed up the next day at her usual time, but she didn't linger to chat as she used to do. She delivered her basket, picked up the empty one and bolted. Luc hoped it was because she was busy and not because she no longer wanted to spend time with him. Even if friendship was all he could hope for, he didn't want to lose that.

The next day it was the same thing. She zoomed in, gravel spraying from her tires, dropped off his order, and was gone. Luc was going into severe withdrawal. He tried to tell himself it was better this way, a clean break, but he couldn't convince himself.

The ache in his chest that wouldn't go away was as alien to him as the spicy Cajun food had been when he'd first moved to Louisiana. He'd gotten used to the food and had come to love it. But the pain of losing Loretta before he'd even really had her—he wasn't sure he could ever get used to that. He was reluctant to analyze what that meant, but the realization that any woman could do this to him was almost more upsetting than the situation itself.

By Saturday he didn't have time to think about Loretta or anyone else other than the guests at La Petite Maison. Every room was full except for the attic suite. By that afternoon, it would be occupied, too. As soon as the breakfast dishes were washed and put away, it was time to get started on lunch. Some of the guests had paid extra for a gourmet picnic under the shade of a two-hundred-year-old live oak. The picnic was another of his experiments, something else he could advertise at the festival.

As he was cleaning up the leftovers after lunch, something caught his eye down on the banks of the bayou. A flash of bright red hair.

His immediate thought was of Loretta, of course. But as he craned his neck and tried to get another glimpse, the figure near the water came into view again and he realized the person was much too small to be Loretta.

Concern for Zara welled up inside him. Should she be playing so close to the water's edge? The bayou was beautiful, but dangerous, too. He hadn't forgotten about the alligator, which could eat Zara in two bites.

He abandoned the picnic leftovers and went to investigate. He came across her purple bike first, lying on its side where she'd left it when the ground got too muddy. Then he found Zara, looking adorable in little overalls and a sunny yellow shirt. Her beautiful hair was unbound. Luc had never seen her without her pigtails.

She squatted near the river's edge, peering at something.

"Zara?"

She turned and saw him, and a big smile lit up her face. "Luc!"

"Hey, gorgeous. Are you here by yourself?"

"I'm a big girl. I don't need a babysitter."

He supposed a nine-year-old could be on her own for short periods, at least in a small town where everyone watched out for each other. But not this close to the bayou.

"What are you doing?" he asked in a nonaccusatory way, just curious.

"Catching crawdads. I'm helping Mama. She said Bryan Givens is giving her fits because he wants to sell her crawdads for her dinner, but he won't say how many or how much they cost."

"Crawdads" were what the locals called crawfish, the tiny, lobsterlike critters that were a mainstay of the Cajun diet. Luc had not developed a taste for them—it was too much work to get that tiny piece of meat out of the shell—and he felt nauseous every time he saw someone sucking on a detached crayfish head, which was what Louisianans did. But the local specialty was an integral part of Loretta's authentic Cajun feast.

"Got one!" Zara announced, and he saw now that she was watching a crayfish mound, into which she'd dropped a string. She slowly pulled on the string until the crayfish popped out. "See, they're so dumb, they latch onto that little bit o' bacon and they won't let go." She grabbed her prize and dropped it into a bucket, where it joined about half a dozen of its neighbors.

Zara would have to catch a few hundred more if she wanted to make a dent in her mother's crawfish requirements, but Luc thought the effort was sweet.

"That's real noble of you to want to help out, but I'm a little worried about you down here by yourself."

"Why? I can swim. Like a fish, Granddaddy says."

He didn't want to scare Zara, but he felt obligated to explain to her about the danger. "I saw an alligator not far from here a few days ago."

But she wasn't afraid. He should have known. "I

want to see the alligator!" She peered hopefully out into the murky water.

"You probably wouldn't be able to see it. It looks just like a log—until it pops out of the water and grabs you."

"Ew."

"How about I fix you a snack? Have you had lunch?"

"No, I sort of forgot. What kind of snack?"

"Brie cheese and grapes?" He had some left over from the picnic. "But you'll have to help me carry in the picnic things."

"Cool. Okay." She grabbed her bucket, and they walked to the live oak tree. There wasn't much left to take in. He gave Zara a plastic sack containing the leftover food, then he gathered up the tablecloth and they walked together up to the cottage.

Some of the guests had gathered on the back veranda to sit in the rocking chairs and enjoy the fine weather. Two older women took one look at Zara and began fawning over her, which she endured stoically. Cute as she was, she probably got this type of attention a lot.

"What's your name, honey?" one woman asked.

"How old are you?"

"What's in the bucket?"

"That's a mighty pretty pair of tennis shoes."

"Don't be shy, now."

After Zara politely answered their questions, one of the ladies looked up at Luc and beamed. "You have a beautiful daughter, and so sweet and bright."

Luc was shocked at the feeling that welled up in

him. In fact, for a split second, it had felt like Zara *was*
his. And he'd experienced a surge of pride—as if she
really were his daughter.

CHAPTER NINE

ZARA GIGGLED but didn't correct the woman.

Luc felt he should. "She's actually the daughter of a friend of mine. But thank you. I'll pass on your compliments to her mother."

Once they were safely inside, Zara laughed again. "That lady thought you were my dad. We don't look anything alike."

"Sometimes parents and their kids don't look alike."

"Do you have any kids?" Zara asked innocently.

"No, I've never been married, so I haven't had the pleasure."

"Oh, so you *want* kids?"

Alarm bells went off in Luc's mind. Maybe Zara's question hadn't been so innocent after all. "I like kids, but I move around a lot. It's kind of hard to be a good dad if you're moving all the time."

"Yeah, my dad—my real dad—was like that," she said, seemingly unconcerned about it. "I don't remember him, and now he's dead."

"My father died a couple of years ago, too." More than three, actually. That hardly seemed possible. His memories of sitting by his father's deathbed were still so clear in his mind. Pierre Robichaux, the man who'd fathered him but had never been much of a father, had asked one thing from Luc.

And Luc, who'd blamed himself for Pierre abandoning his family, had been all too eager to follow Pierre's wishes. Fueled by his anger over the way his father's family had treated him—relying far too heavily on Pierre's version of the truth—Luc had crossed a line he wished he hadn't.

Which was how he'd ended up here in Indigo.

"Wash your hands, please, Zara."

She complied, barely able to reach the kitchen sink. He put a wedge of Brie cheese and grapes onto a small plate, then added some crackers and a spreading knife.

"So why do you move around so much?" Zara asked.

"I don't know," he answered honestly. "It's just what I do. I've been all over the world and I haven't seen a thousandth of the amazing things that I hope to see."

"Well, I see amazing things here in Indigo every day, and I don't even have to travel. I even saw an ivory-billed woodpecker once, but no one believes me 'cept my mom." Zara settled into a chair at the wrought iron table and surveyed the feast. "Is this Brie cheese?"

"Yup. If you don't like it, I have some cheddar."

"Oh, no, this will do fine. I'm not a fussy eater. My mom says I'm easy to feed. You can give me any old kind of leftovers."

Uh-huh. Luc had a sneaky suspicion he knew where this conversation was going, but he had no idea how to head it off.

"In fact, I'm not much trouble at all."

"Except when you get in fights at school," he reminded her.

"I quit fighting."

Luc stole a couple of grapes off her plate and munched on them. Had he eaten lunch? He'd been so busy, he couldn't remember. He stretched and put his hands behind his head, just enjoying this time with Zara. He was curious to see where she'd go next.

"So when are you leaving Indigo?" she asked.

"Not till next spring." In April, his two-year probation would be over. Another three years staying out of trouble, and his record would be expunged. He'd gotten off easy, considering.

"Why then?"

"Well, by then I'll have finished all the rebuilding work on La Petite Maison, and it'll be running smoothly. My grandmother owns this place, see, and she hired me to fix it up and start the B and B. But when the job's done…" He shrugged.

"You'll just leave?"

"That's the plan."

"Where will you go?"

He hadn't given it much thought. He never was one to make elaborate plans—and look what had happened the one time he did. "I thought maybe I'd go to Italy."

Her nose crinkled. "But won't you miss us?" Zara's attempt to make it sound like a casual question fell way short.

"Of course I'll miss you. I've made lots of good friends here."

"So why don't you stay? Your grandmother would let you keep working here, I bet."

He wasn't so sure about that. By forcing him to work here, Celeste was getting her pound of flesh out of him. If she figured out that he actually liked it here, she would probably fire him instantly.

"It's just not in me, Zara. I'm a rolling stone. I have to keep moving."

Like his father? He recalled a particular conversation between his parents, right before Pierre had left for the last time. Luc couldn't have been more than six, but he remembered it clearly. Pierre had said pretty much the same thing Luc had just said to Zara—that he wasn't good at sticking around, that he had to keep moving.

His mother's most fervent wish was that Luc *not* turn out like Pierre. And he'd obliged her by never drinking excessively or gambling. But was he becoming his father in other ways? He couldn't imagine abandoning his own wife and child as Pierre had done. Then again, he couldn't imagine getting married and having a child to begin with.

Or could he? How much of that rolling-stone personality was ingrained, and how much of it was manufactured in some misguided need to have something in common with his father?

Zara didn't much care for his reasoning. "You *could* stay in one place, if you really wanted to."

If he didn't get ridden out of town on a rail, tarred and feathered, which probably would happen if he hurt Loretta. "That's true, Zara. We all have free will. We can decide what we want to do with our lives, where we want to live and who we want to live with. To some degree."

"So don't you like my mama? Wouldn't you stay here for her?"

The child was tying him in knots. Talk about a master manipulator. How did one answer a question like that? "Zara, I think the world of you and your mother. And I also want what's best for you. Even if I wanted to settle down in one place…it's very complex."

"That's what grown-ups say when they think I can't understand something. But if you'd just explain it, maybe I *would* understand."

How could he explain it when he didn't understand it himself? He wanted to be with Loretta, but he couldn't offer any guarantees, and she needed guarantees. Which meant that for her own good, he needed to stay away from her.

He couldn't tell that to a nine-year-old.

"It's 'cause of me, right?" Zara asked in a small voice. "Guys don't like single mothers. They don't want kids who don't belong to them getting in the way."

"Where did you hear that?"

"On TV."

"Well, it's not true, not of me, anyway. I consider you a plus. When that lady on the veranda thought you were my daughter, I sort of liked it," he confessed.

"Then how come—"

"Zara. You're just going to have to trust your mother and me on this one. As smart as you are, there are things you don't understand. I can't marry your mom. I can't be your dad."

He hated himself for being so blunt. But he could see now why Loretta was worried. Zara had apparently invested quite a bit in this happily-ever-after fantasy of hers. Better to dash her hopes now than let them get more out of hand.

Zara didn't say anything for a couple of minutes. She spent a long time spreading cheese onto a cracker, covering every square millimeter of its surface in an even coating.

She was trying not to cry.

He'd never felt so powerless. Whatever pain she felt, he felt it ten times over.

"It looks like it might rain," he said after a while. A lame attempt to change the subject.

To his surprise, it worked. Zara cast a worried look out the window. "I better start for home," she said dully. "Mama hates it when I get caught in the rain. She thinks I'll get sick. But if getting wet makes you sick, how come people take baths?"

He had to laugh. She was such a funny kid. "That is a very good question."

She took her plate to the sink. "Thank you for the snack."

"You're most welcome."

"I still like you."

His heart constricted. "And I still like you. A whole lot."

She surprised him by giving him a quick, fierce hug. Then she ran out the back door.

He stepped out onto the porch to watch as she ran down toward the area where she'd left her bike. The sky had grown very dark, and as she hopped onto the bike and started pedaling, the skies opened up. She gave a little shriek as the cold rain hit, and he motioned for her to take shelter with him.

The rain fell in sheets.

"I think you better wait this one out."

"I can't. It's almost time for my fiddle lesson with Chief Boudreaux, and I can't be late. We're working on my song for the music festival."

He'd have offered to throw her bike in the back of the Tahoe and run her home, but he didn't feel right leaving when he had a house full of guests. "How about if I call your mom? She can bring your fiddle and take you to Alain's house." Although Luc and Loretta lived at opposite ends of Indigo, the drive was less than five minutes.

"Okay. But she hates to close the bakery on a Saturday."

"It'll just be for a few minutes." And he didn't mind having yet another excuse to call Loretta. He was a masochist.

"Indigo Bakery." Luc barely recognized Loretta's voice on the phone, she sounded so harried.

"Loretta?"

"Oh, Luc. I thought it was Bryan about the crayfish again. If he weren't local, and if our kids weren't in Girl Explorers together, I'd get my crawdads somewhere else." She paused for breath. "Sorry. I'm a woman obsessed. Do you need to change tomorrow's order?"

"No. I have something of yours."

"You do?" She sounded bewildered. "What?"

"Zara. She rode her bike over, and now she's stranded—"

"Zara's with you?" Her voice sounded just this side of panicky.

"She's fine."

"I didn't even know she was gone! My God, it's almost two o'clock! I haven't checked on her in hours. What kind of mother am I?"

"Loretta, take it easy. She's fine, but it's pouring rain and she's worried about her fiddle lesson."

"I'll be right over to get her. And tell her she's in trouble. She knows she isn't supposed to leave the house without telling me where she's going." She hung up.

Well, wasn't that warm and fuzzy. "She said you're in trouble," he told Zara solemnly.

"I am?" Zara looked puzzled. "'Cause I came to see you?"

"Because you didn't tell her where you were going."

Zara drew herself up. "Yes, I did! I told her I was going to catch crawdads." She sighed. "Mama doesn't remember anything. She tried to get me up for school today, and it's Saturday." She gnawed on her lower lip.

"Your mom has a lot on her mind right now. Speaking of forgetting things, you better get your crawdads. You left the bucket on the back porch."

Zara gasped. "I did forget! Maybe it's catching." And she ran through the house like a miniature hellion. Luc ached to think about the hearts she would break.

By the time Zara returned with her bucket, Loretta's station wagon had pulled up the drive. She must've broken the speed limit to get here.

She shot out of the car like a bullet.

"She looks mad," Zara said under her breath.

She looked possessed. "Zara Castille. I'd like to be able to say I was worried sick about you, but since I didn't know you were gone—"

"Mama," Zara said with exaggerated patience, "I did tell you where I was going. I said I was gonna ride my bike to the bayou and catch crawdads, remember?"

Loretta opened her mouth to argue back, then clamped it shut.

"You're right. You did tell me. I was in the middle of adding a column of numbers. Oh, baby, I'm so sorry." She leaned down to hug Zara, and Zara hugged her back. "I'm such a bad mom. I should spend more time with you."

"Mama, I'm gonna miss my fiddle lesson. The rain's stopped. Can I ride my bike now?"

Sure enough, the rain had stopped as quickly as it had started. "Just be careful. The roads are slick."

"I will." She dashed to get her fiddle case out of the car, then laid it carefully in the wicker basket on her bike's handlebars. "Bye, Luc," she said with a cheerful wave, having recovered her spirits, for which he was grateful. He still felt like the worst of heels for almost making her cry.

"What was she doing here?" Loretta asked.

"Well, she *said* she was here to catch crawdads." He pointed to the bucket, where the seven unfortunate crustaceans languished in an inch of brown water. "But I think her true purpose was to ask my intentions toward you."

Loretta's hand went to her mouth, stifling a gasp. "What did you say?"

"I told her you and I…that it wasn't meant to be."

Loretta rubbed the back of her neck. "I guess she needed to hear it from both of us. She was okay, wasn't she?"

"She almost cried. I feel horrible."

"It's not your fault."

"I never had a little girl want me for a daddy before. It's a weird feeling. Humbling. She's an amazing child, Loretta. You're so lucky to have her."

"I know. And I'm a terrible mother."

"Will you stop saying that?"

"How much time do you think would have passed before I missed her? I didn't feed her lunch, I forgot all about her fiddle lesson."

"And you forgot your own lunch, too, I'll bet."

Loretta put a hand to her flat stomach. "I guess I did."

Luc grabbed her arm and dragged her inside. "I'm feeding you, no arguments. You're a mess, you know that? You're completely stressed out."

She didn't argue. She followed him meekly, sat where he instructed, and let him wait on her. This time he added baked chicken to the Brie and grapes and fixed himself a small plate, too.

"I'm overwhelmed," she admitted after stripping most of the meat from a chicken breast and eating like a starving woman. "I thought I could handle coordinating the food and the dinner, but it's too much for me. Just because I can bake a loaf of bread doesn't mean I know how to do this job. I'm not good with numbers— it's a wonder the bakery isn't bankrupt, the way I keep my financial records."

"You're trying to do the work of an entire committee by yourself, in addition to running a business and raising a daughter. No wonder you're overstretched. Let me help. Why don't you concentrate on the vendors and let me worry about the dinner?"

He could tell she wanted to accept his offer, but she hesitated.

"It's called delegating. As a committee chair, you're allowed to do that. You can bring me up to speed tomorrow at our meeting."

She looked like a bunny about to get snagged by a hawk. "Meeting?"

"To plan our booth?"

"Oh. Oh, right. I've completely lost my memory."

"Stress will do that to you. Let me deal with some of your problems. Hell, let *me* talk to Bryan. You'll have a firm price on those crawfish in no time."

"Really?"

"I know how to deal with difficult vendors."

"Why?"

"Why? Because I've been in the hotel business for—"

"No, I mean, why are you being so nice to me? When I've been perfectly horrible to you? Fickle and flaky and inconsiderate—"

"I thought you were done beating up on yourself."

She looked down at her lap. "*Someone's* responsible for the mess I'm making of my life these days."

"I'm offering to help because I can't stand to see you unhappy. You or Zara. I want to see you smile."

She reached over and took his hand, squeezing it

hard. "I'll accept your offer, then." When she looked up, her smile reminded him of the sun when it came out after a brief storm—intense enough to warm his cold heart.

Suddenly, he realized there *was* something that could keep him in one place, something that could stop him from wanting to roam the world. Something that was better than anything he might find in the far corners of the earth.

Loretta's smile.

CHAPTER TEN

LORETTA FELT SOMETHING go *ca-thunk* inside her chest.
Why was Luc looking at her that way? And why
couldn't she stop looking at him?

And why was she still holding on to his hand when
she'd only meant to give it a squeeze?

The space in Luc's kitchen seemed to shrink to the
few cubic feet they occupied. Everything in her periph-
eral vision faded until there was only Luc's face, with
his slightly crooked nose and the scar on his chin and
the sandy hair in need of a trim. It was a handsome face,
filled with character and wisdom beyond his years.

She couldn't stop herself. She reached up with her
free hand to touch his cheek, as if she could hold on to
that character and capture some of that wisdom for
herself.

"Loretta…" The single word dripped with caution.
But he didn't pull away. "We just made a difficult
decision, you and I, not to do this."

"I know."

"I'm trying to come to terms with it. So is Zara."

Now he was pulling out the big guns. "I know."

"I do not have enough willpower to say no to you."

"Good." She literally threw herself at him, kissing him with the longing and desperation that had been building inside her for days. It was no good denying herself, it just made her crazy. His response was not gentle. He stood and yanked her up so he could press her against the refrigerator. He kissed her like a crazy man, running his hands up and down her body. Her nipples hardened painfully against her bra.

"This is not fair to either one of us," he said.

"I'll make it fair. Any terms you want. I can't stand it anymore. Please, where's your bedroom?"

That put an end to his arguments. He swung her up into his arms and strode out of the kitchen and into a small suite of rooms that were obviously his living quarters. The décor was far more Spartan here than in the rest of the house, with white walls, a pine dresser and a plain iron bed.

It was the bed she focused on. There was no shy striptease, no laughter, no hesitation of any kind. She wanted possession. If loving Luc was wrong, then she didn't want to do the right thing, the sensible thing.

He very nearly tore her clothes off, and did manage to pop a button on her blouse. It pinged across the bare cypress floor. Even as he stripped off her clothes, he kept kissing her…hot, undisciplined kisses. She felt no embarrassment, only a sense that this moment was preordained.

She wanted Luc. She wanted him for as long as he would have her.

He lifted her up and practically threw her onto his bed, the sweet, pastel-colored antique quilt a sharp contrast to the intensity of their feelings.

"Don't move." He stepped into the bathroom and came back out holding a plastic bag from a pharmacy in New Iberia. "After I left your place last week, I drove all the way to New Iberia to get these." He dropped a large box of condoms onto the bed. He was letting her know, in no uncertain terms, that he'd had plans for the two of them, plans she'd ruined.

She knew she couldn't change her mind again. Maybe Luc wasn't the settling-down, marrying type, but that didn't mean he had a heart of stone.

"We'll use them all."

At that, the last of his anger dissipated. He shucked his jeans and fell on top of her. The weight of him, his heat, his pure maleness met a need in her she couldn't describe, hadn't known existed until this moment.

She wanted him now, hot and fast. She knew he was ready—kind of hard to miss. She spread her legs and rocked side to side until he was settled between them. Grabbing one of the condoms, she ripped open the package with her teeth and handed it to him. "Do it now."

Her hunger excited him. His eyes darkened, and she strained her hips upward to meet him, to urge him on. He plunged inside her.

"Oh, yes." Finally. Maybe she would be able to sleep tonight.

For a time he didn't move as they adjusted to the feel of their bodies joined. But then he began to thrust, short, subtle movements at first, building to long, deep insertions, withdrawing almost all the way, then coming home to her again. Hard, hot, intense. She thought she might weep with the ecstasy of it.

He gritted his teeth, sweat running down his face.

"I'm coming," he whispered. "Can't…hold…it…"

And neither could she. She felt herself come apart, and for a time she wasn't sure where her body was. Not under her control, that's for sure.

Gradually she became aware of the soft quilt against her back and Luc's warm skin on hers.

"Hmm."

"Is that all you have to say?" she demanded, though she was teasing. "Hmm?"

"Sorta defies words. That was, uh…see? No words." He pulled away from her and flopped onto his back next to her, then drew her close.

"How about good?"

"Doesn't come close."

"Spectacular?"

"Better than that."

"Worth repeating?"

He grinned. "Now you're getting somewhere. Does your mother know you behave like this?"

"She better not."

Luc stroked her cheek and smoothed her hair off her forehead. "I didn't mean to be rough."

"You didn't hurt me. I'm not made of spun sugar."

They lay in silence for a while. Loretta knew they had to talk about what this meant. Denying their attraction hadn't worked. They needed a new plan. A plan that included frequent and hot sex.

"You want a relationship?" she asked. "A real one?"

"Yes," he said without hesitation. "I don't want to sneak around. Zara has to know."

"Okay."

"She's smart. I say we tell her the absolute truth."

"What is the absolute truth?"

"That I'm crazy about you. Right now, I can't imagine wanting to leave Indigo. But I know myself. I'm restless. I have too much of my father in me."

"Tell me about your father."

Luc smiled, a little sadly, it seemed to Loretta. "I think he loved my mother and me. The way he looked at her sometimes—I could tell. But he didn't stick around. Even when I was very young, he disappeared for long periods of time—weeks, months sometimes. Then he'd show back up, his arms full of presents, making all kinds of promises about how it would be different this time. It never was. Always, he would leave again.

"Eventually, my mother had had enough, and she told him if he left again, not to bother coming back. He left, anyway, and my mom divorced him. I was six, I think."

Loretta could tell it was not easy for Luc to talk about this.

"He came back, just before he died," he said. "He wanted to make peace. He had hepatitis, the serious kind. We took care of him till he died."

"I'm sorry."

"I don't want to repeat his mistakes. I don't want to make promises I can't keep. Do you understand?"

"Yes, I think so. And I'm willing to accept your…limitations. Can we just take it one day at a time, see how it goes? If it doesn't work out in the long run, if you feel you have to leave, I'll be sad, but I won't regret our time together."

"I hope not. I wouldn't hurt you for anything. Or Zara. How about if we talk to her together?"

"Okay." She smiled up at him, the sweetest, most heartbreaking smile, and he kissed her.

LUC COULD HARDLY believe he was lying there talking so calmly about having a relationship. And that it didn't panic him in the least.

The doorbell rang. Luc looked at his watch and cursed softly. "That would be my guests. Sorry." He gave her one more quick kiss, then leaped out of bed and quickly put on his clothes.

"Do you mind if I take a shower?" Loretta asked him.

"No, go ahead. Make yourself at home."

Luc tucked in his shirt as he headed for the front door. The doorbell rang again—someone was growing impatient.

"I'm coming," he grumbled. "Sheesh." He opened the door, but it wasn't the couple from Mobile he'd been expecting. Standing on the front porch was Celeste Robichaux, looking like a dowager duchess. *"Grand-mère?"*

"What took you so long?" she demanded, sweeping past him and into the house. "And why do you keep the door locked? We never locked the door when we used to stay here."

"I'm a city boy. Locking doors is a habit with me." Out in the driveway, a tall, gaunt man in a uniform stood at the back of Celeste's Cadillac, pulling out enough suitcases for a trip around the world.

Oh, boy.

Celeste stood in the middle of the main room and looked around, taking in the furnishings, the pictures on the wall, the rag rugs and the fragrant potpourri, and Luc held his breath. Would she like what she saw? Had he really caught the essence from the few old photos he'd discovered?

Her face softened. "Oh, Luc, this is fabulous. It looks almost exactly as it did when I was a girl. You've worked a miracle, an absolute miracle."

"I'm glad you like it." Wow. Praise from Celeste. This was a red-letter day.

The chauffeur carried in Celeste's suitcases and one large box.

"Charles," she said, "take everything but the box up to the third floor. Luc, you did say the attic suite had a private bath, correct?"

"*Grand-mère,* as happy as I am to see you, you can't stay here. I'm full up. Guests will be arriving any minute who've reserved the attic suite."

"Well, you'll just have to put them someplace else. This is my house, I ought to be able to stay here when I want. Charles?" She nodded toward the stairs.

"Yes, ma'am." He gave Luc a commiserating look before heading up the stairs with the baggage.

"I'd like the grand tour, please. Show me everything you've done."

The door to Luc's private quarters opened and Loretta stepped out, wearing his bathrobe. "Luc? Sorry to bother you, but I can't get any hot water. Is there a trick to it?" She nodded toward Celeste. "Hi."

"Good afternoon," Celeste said, giving Luc a look designed to turn him into a pile of ashes. "This must be Loretta."

Loretta's eyebrows flew up. She'd apparently mistaken Celeste for a guest.

"*Grand-mère,* I'd like you to meet Loretta Castille. She's our local baker. Loretta, my grandmother, Celeste Robichaux."

Loretta came forward, her hand extended, though her face had turned bright pink. Celeste took her hand reluctantly, gave it a quick shake and let go.

"It's nice to meet you, Mrs. Robichaux," Loretta said.

"The hot water just takes a while to heat up," Luc said.

"Okay, thanks." And she fled.

"Well, well," Celeste said. "Looks like she's providing you with more than muffins. I hope you're not flaunting your little floozy in front of the guests."

"No, ma'am. But she's not a floozy, and please don't call her that. She's my girlfriend." He liked the sound of that.

"I didn't know you had a steady girlfriend."

"It's a relatively new thing."

"Mmm-hmm." She pressed her mouth into a stern line, obviously displeased. Just as he thought, she'd been hoping he was miserable in Indigo. He was making restitution here. He wasn't supposed to be enjoying himself.

As he took her around and showed her the rooms in the old Creole cottage, though, her disapproving frown faded.

"I had no idea you'd be so good at decorating."

"Doc helped. He remembered what the cottage was like years ago, so he helped me find furniture and rugs." Luc had enjoyed spiffing the place up and including little touches he knew the guests would appreciate— like a basket of fresh fruit in the parlor and woolly afghans to wrap themselves in when they sat on the porch on a chilly night.

When Celeste went out on one of the balconies and saw the cypress rocking chairs, she sat in one. "We used to have mint juleps out here on warm days, and mulled wine or cider on cold ones. It was such a wonderful time, especially the summers. We had parties and picnics and boat rides. And on Saturday afternoons all the young people would drive to New Iberia to the movie house."

Celeste was actually smiling. Luc had never seen her like this. He could almost envision the beautiful young girl she'd once been.

"How long are you planning to stay?" he asked.

"Oh, just a couple of weeks. Maybe until the music festival. I've heard so much about it now, since Melanie is involved."

Luc resisted the urge to clutch his chest. Two weeks! Or longer? God almighty, this was awful.

"Do you even like Cajun music?" he asked.

"But *oui.* Back in my day there were some good bands. In fact, I had a, er, gentleman friend who played the *frottoir* in a band."

Luc didn't know what a *"frottoir"* was, but he remembered hearing the word before somewhere.

"There was a little bandstand set up on the lawn in front of the opera house," Celeste continued, "and they would play every evening, and the young people would dance. The old people, too, come to think of it."

Man. He had never imagined...

The doorbell rang again. What was he going to do with his guests? He'd been working on converting one of the outbuildings to a suite, but it wasn't quite ready.

When he went to the door, however, it wasn't his guests, but Doc Landry. "Hey, Doc. Why didn't you just let yourself in?" Doc had a key, since he often watched the B and B when Luc was away.

"Oh, well, it just seems more proper to ring the bell when I wasn't expected. Do you, uh, have a special guest?" And he looked past Luc, searching.

"You must mean *Grand-mère*. Oh, yeah, she's here, all right."

"I thought that was her car leaving just now."

It was hard to miss Celeste's car. She had vanity plates that said, "QUEEN C." Luc couldn't help grinning. His cousins' no longer secret nickname for their grandmother was "The Queen."

Loretta picked that moment to emerge from Luc's rooms, fully dressed this time, thank God. "Hi, Doc," she said. Then she whispered, "I hope I didn't get you in trouble with your grandmother."

"I'm always in trouble with my grandmother."

"I need to get back to the bakery."

"I'll call you later." In full view of Doc, he kissed her goodbye. Doc would find out soon enough.

"Well," Doc said when Loretta had left.

"Don't give me grief, okay?"

Celeste came down the stairs and smiled broadly when she saw her old friend. "Well, look who's here. Michel, the years have been kind to you."

"And to you." Doc stepped forward, took Celeste's hand, and kissed it. "You're as beautiful as ever."

Michel? Luc wasn't sure he'd ever been aware of Doc Landry's first name. Everyone called him Doc. Then Luc remembered where he'd heard about the *frottoir.* From Doc. Hmm.

Doc lifted the plastic bag in his hand. "Everything we need for mint juleps. Are you game?"

"I haven't had a mint julep in years. My doctor will have a fit, but I'd love one. I believe I even saw the perfect cocktail glasses in the china cabinet."

Shaking his head, Luc left his grandmother in very capable hands to see what he could do about the out-building. He'd already made the necessary changes to plumbing and wiring. He'd made repairs on the roof, replaced one of the windows, painted, and bought a bed and dresser. He'd installed a claw-foot tub in the bathroom, but he hadn't yet done a shower conversion. Most hotel guests loved the old tubs, but they wanted to take showers.

He could make the room do, he supposed. He quickly put some linens on the bed and towels in the bathroom, and borrowed a few pictures, knickknacks, and a rug to make it more homey. The results weren't up to his usual standards, but they would have to do.

When the couple from Mobile finally arrived just before dinner, he explained about the unexpected arrival of his grandmother, who owned the place. Then he showed them the outbuilding.

The woman was delighted with what she called the "rustic character" of the place, but the man was not pleased, until Luc mentioned that he was giving them a substantial discount on the room rate. That solved the problem.

When Luc returned to the main house, he joined his guests on the downstairs veranda, where Doc was serving mint juleps to everyone. He handed Luc a glass.

"Come, sit with us," Doc said.

"I have a lot of work to—"

"Sit."

Oh, boy. He dragged up one of the rocking chairs and sat gingerly on the edge, making it clear he wasn't settling in for the evening.

"You told me you were going to leave Loretta alone," Doc said without preamble.

"Now, Michel," Celeste chided, "are you saying my grandson isn't good enough for this girl?"

This was a switch. Celeste defending him?

"I just don't want to see the girl hurt," Doc said. "She's been through a lot in her young life already."

A couple of the guests, seated nearby, were eavesdropping. Luc wanted to sink through the veranda. "I'm not sure this is anybody's business but mine," he said softly. "But I have to tell you, Loretta and I have reached an understanding. I'm happy with it, she's happy, and frankly I don't care too much what you two think."

"All right, all right, simmer down," Doc said. "I just

want to know one thing. Does she know about your, er, past?"

"No," Luc admitted.

"Oh, Luc, you have to tell her," Celeste said. "She has a right to know, especially what with her late husband being a criminal and all."

It seemed Doc had filled Celeste in.

"I'll tell her. I just have to find the right time. She's so busy with the music festival, so stressed out, I don't want to spring the news that her new boyfriend is a…" He stopped and looked pointedly at one of the female guests who was craning her neck, trying to hear.

"*Grand-mère,* you won't say anything, will you?" He imagined Celeste would take great pleasure in relating Luc's felony record to Loretta. She seemed to enjoy manipulating the members of her family.

She answered his question with one of her own. "Do you love her?"

"I can't answer that." If the ache in his chest every time he saw her was love, then maybe he did. But he suspected what Celeste meant was, did he plan to make an honest woman out of her.

"I would highly recommend telling her the truth," Celeste said. "As soon as possible. I won't say anything, if that's what you want. But sooner or later she will find out from someone else."

"No one else knows except for the police chief. Do they, Doc?"

"I haven't told anyone."

"What about Melanie?" Celeste asked.

Oh, hell. He'd forgotten about Melanie. "I'll talk to

her. It's just for another couple of weeks. I need that time with Loretta." Maybe it was selfish of him. But there was a very good chance Loretta would bolt the moment she found out that Luc had plotted revenge against his own family and had nearly succeeded in destroying their hotel. He wanted at least a little time with her before she knew the truth.

CELESTE WAS ON HER third mint julep and feeling no pain. Sitting on the veranda like this, rocking and laughing and feeling the breeze on her face, she could almost believe she was young again. Young and wealthy and carefree, with a world of choices unfolding before her.

"What do you really think of Luc's new girlfriend?" she asked Michel. Luc had gone inside to prepare a cold buffet for some of his guests. Usually people chose to drive to New Iberia or St. Martinville for dinner, or they enjoyed a homestyle meal at Indigo's own Blue Moon Diner, but he'd given them the option of eating at the B and B tonight.

He was really very good at what he did. Her idea to have him renovate the cabin and open a bed-and-breakfast had been smarter than even she'd imagined.

"Loretta's a peach," Doc said. "She comes from a good family. It's true, she made some bad choices in her youth. She couldn't have picked a worse husband than Jim Patterson. But she grew up and settled down. She's putting all her energy into her bakery and making a success of it, too. And she's a good mother."

"Mother?" Celeste sat up straighter. "You didn't tell me she had a child."

"Must've slipped my mind. Zara. She's, oh, about nine now, I think. Smart as a whip and quite a handful. A lot like her mother was at that age."

"It's hard for me to picture Luc dating a single mother. It seems so…responsible. Not at all like his father." She pursed her lips, thinking about her son, Pierre. After the brouhaha in New Orleans and finding out Luc was Pierre's son, she'd assumed the two had much in common.

But maybe not as much as she'd originally thought.

"Luc *is* responsible," Doc assured her. "Maybe his brush with the law made him see the light, but I'd trust him with my life. He adores Zara. He'd make a fine daddy."

"Hmph. Raising children is no picnic. In fact, I'd say it's the hardest, most challenging job in the world. I certainly didn't excel at it."

"How can you say that? You raised a fine daughter."

Celeste smiled. "Anne turned out wonderfully. I've only recently begun to appreciate what a strong, special woman she is. But not through my doing. She bloomed despite my attempts to control her. But Pierre—he didn't fare as well."

"We all do the best we can, Celeste. You have to let that one go."

"I've made so many mistakes."

"We all have."

"Not you. You married a nice woman who never gave you a bit of trouble. You built a wonderful life for yourself. I married someone I didn't love because I could control him, and because he could give me the lifestyle I wanted."

"Water under the bridge, my dear," Doc soothed her. "Water under the bridge."

CHAPTER ELEVEN

LORETTA WASN'T SURE what had changed. She still had a mess on her hands, with too many food vendors and not enough space. She still wasn't completely happy with her artisanal breads and couldn't figure out exactly how she would promote her bakery at the festival. But her problems didn't seem quite so serious now.

She couldn't believe that an hour of wild sex could make such a huge difference in her life. But after she came home from Luc's and returned to her baking, everything seemed different. She was relaxed. She felt a sense of peace. She was able to add up columns of numbers with ease, and her formerly unmanageable budget didn't seem like such a bear.

Even Zara sensed Loretta's new attitude. "Did anything happen while I was at my fiddle lesson?" she asked innocently.

Loretta tensed. "What do you mean?"

"You just seem happier. You're not psycho like you were this morning."

"Zara, it's not nice to refer to your mother as psycho, even if she is."

"Sorry. How about whacko?"

"I'm just feeling like I have things under control, now that Luc has promised to help me with my music festival stuff. We're going to meet tomorrow at Grandma and Granddaddy's house to work out all the details. Oh, and he's going to get my crawdads from Bryan at a decent price—he promised."

"That's good, because I left the ones I caught at Luc's."

Loretta's serenity lasted only until the following afternoon, when the meeting actually took place, because Luc's grandmother came with him. She'd invited herself, apparently. The woman was eighty-five years old—she announced this herself almost before introductions were over—yet she was remarkably well-preserved. Although slightly stooped, she was slim and vibrated with energy. She had gorgeous bone structure and clear, smooth skin. She wore her silver hair in a French roll, a jeweled comb adorning it.

Her sharp, darting eyes seemed to miss nothing.

Luc carried in a large box, and they all settled in the living room. Adele Castille fixed them all sweet iced tea and served cookies, and Celeste seemed to appreciate the civility of it. She managed not to get a single crumb on anything.

"Now, then, Luc," Celeste said, taking control of the meeting, "if you'll open that box, there are some things I wish to show you all."

Luc followed directions, and the first thing he pulled out was a sort of presentation album. Celeste laid it on the coffee table and opened it. "I took the liberty of having my interior designer draw up some plans for the booth. Now, don't worry about the expense. We can borrow a few things from the B and B."

Loretta almost fainted at the lavish drawing. Celeste wanted to deck out their booth like the Taj Mahal.

"It's beautiful," she said, meaning it. "But I'm afraid our space isn't that big."

"Then how are we going to display all the pictures?" Celeste nodded at the box.

Luc began pulling photographs and news clippings out of the box—some of them framed, some not. They were a treasure trove of Indigo history, dating back as early as the Civil War. There were even pictures from the old Indigo plantations that had given the town its name, and each was meticulously described and dated.

"My family has always been interested in history," Celeste explained. "These pictures belonged mostly to my father. Blanchards have been a part of Indigo's history for hundreds of years. This music festival is the perfect opportunity to highlight that history—and the history of the whole town, of course," she added.

Loretta marveled at the pictures a few moments longer. She found photos of the B and B—the huge oak trees that surrounded it now had been much smaller—and some of the opera house.

"Hey," Vincent said, "there's my grandfather! He captained a mail boat that ran up and down the Bayou Teche way back when."

Just then, Loretta got a brainstorm. "What if we used this idea for the opera house, instead of our booth? People are going to be touring the building anyway, and there will be some performers there. We could make the second-floor gallery into a temporary museum. And we could give you the credit, Mrs. Robichaux. We could make up a plaque."

Celeste seemed pleased. "I was thinking of donating these things to the town to start a collection of some sort. I have letters and some other museum-quality artifacts, too."

Adele clapped her hands together, excited as a child. "That would be wonderful! And so educational for the children." She was a retired schoolteacher who still volunteered at the school.

"Um, not to be a wet blanket," Luc said, "but who's going to make all this happen? Loretta and I have our hands full with coordinating the food."

"I'll do it," Adele said, full of enthusiasm. "I have too much time on my hands, anyway. With your input, of course, Mrs. Robichaux. And we'll have to get the cooperation of Marjolaine Savoy, who's coordinating the festival. But she's also on the committee to resurrect the opera house, so I can't imagine she'll object."

Celeste obviously enjoyed being deferred to. "We can work together. Perhaps we can form our own committee. I'll bet Michel would enjoy working on this, as well."

"Who is Michel?" Adele asked.

"I believe you all know him as 'Doc.'"

Did Celeste's eyes sparkle just a bit at the mention of the town's charming doctor? Oh, surely that was just Loretta's imagination.

"What about the booth?" Luc objected. "Promoting our businesses? Wasn't that the point?"

But Celeste seemed less interested in a booth now that she had a better plan for showcasing her family history. "Whatever you think is best, Luc. You know the hotel business better than me. Mrs. Castille, shall we walk over to the opera house and have a look at the space? Perhaps Miss Savoy would join us."

"Great idea," Adele said. "I'll get my camera and a tape measure. And please, call me Adele."

Zara popped in, out of breath from playing outside with the Castilles' Labrador retriever, Bubba. "Mama, can I go to the opera house with Grandma and Mrs. Robichaux?"

Loretta struggled for a reason to say no. Probably Mrs. Robichaux wouldn't want to be distracted by a small child. But before she could answer, Celeste spoke up.

"By all means, child, come with us. I daresay you can stand to learn a bit more about your town's history."

"Oh, I know lots about history, 'cause Grandma is a teacher."

"Zara, don't contradict your elders," Loretta said.

But Celeste was smiling. "I can tell you a few things you would never learn in school."

"I'll bet she has a few stories, too," Vincent said after the trio left through the front door. "In the summers, when the Blanchards and Robichauxs were still using the summer house, I used to hang out with Pierre. We were just little kids, but we found more ways to get in trouble. And your grandmother, no offense, used to scare the bejeezus out of me."

"You knew my father?" Luc leaned forward in his chair, eyes keen with interest.

"Your father?" Vincent repeated. "You mean Pierre? Oh. I didn't make the connection. I mean, I knew you were Celeste's grandson, but I thought you were one of Anne's kids."

"I was just wondering what my father was like as a kid," Luc said. "I didn't know him very well. He didn't hang around long."

"Oh, Pierre, he was a hot-headed one. Always with the big ideas, big plans. Everyone liked him, and he could draw anyone into his schemes. The girls, they especially liked him." Vincent studied Luc. "You look a little bit like him. Not your coloring. But something about your eyes, and the shape of your chin."

Luc rubbed his chin self-consciously. "Maybe we should get back to planning the booth."

Loretta's heart ached for Luc, for the father he never quite had and the obvious hole it had left in his life. Zara often expressed curiosity about her absent father, and Loretta answered her questions as honestly as she could. But it was only recently that she'd begun to sense a yearning in her, too.

Maybe it was only now that her little girl fully realized what she was missing.

THE PLANNING of the booth went fairly smoothly. Loretta and Luc decided to drape colorful fabric as a backdrop and would each have a banner made bearing their logo. Luc would have brochures and photos on hand, and a raffle for a free weekend stay at the B and

B, while Loretta and her father would offer free samples as well as sell their goods. When they'd nailed down the details, Vincent left to tend to his bees.

Luc and Loretta moved to the back porch, where a pillowed porch swing allowed them to take in the setting sun and the muted autumn colors of the woods and the beehives.

Luc wasted no time in pulling Loretta into his arms and kissing her. "I've been waiting all day to do that."

"Me, too. I'm going to tell my parents tonight at dinner that we're…you know. Seeing each other."

"You probably won't have to tell them. Not your mother, anyway. *Grand-mère* will fill her in."

Loretta gasped. "I forgot all about that—she saw me prancing around in your bathrobe. But she wouldn't gossip, would she? Seems like she has more manners than that."

"She'll say whatever it takes to make everyone around her as uncomfortable as possible. That's her mission in life."

"Really? She doesn't strike me that way. A little starchy, maybe…"

"Starchy? That woman is so mean—" But he stopped himself. That was his father talking. Pierre had filled Luc's head with stories about his mother, about how manipulative she was, how cruel. He said she'd virtually kicked him out from the bosom of his family and cheated him out of what was rightfully his.

But after spending time with the Marchands—his Aunt Anne and her daughters—he'd realized how wrong Pierre had been. Anne had grieved for her missing brother and had spent a lot of time, energy and money trying to track him down. And apparently her husband Remy had given Pierre a huge sum of money to pay off his gambling debts in the Cayman Islands, something Pierre had never mentioned.

Luc even had to admit that Celeste was not the monster Pierre had described.

"What is it?" Loretta asked.

"She's not mean," Luc corrected himself. "But she is controlling, and she expects people to fall into line behind her no matter what. She might feel it's her duty to inform your mother of our, um, whatever you want to call it."

"It's a relationship, Luc. Does that word scare you?"

He laughed. "No. That just seems such a lofty word when this is all so new."

"Well, it's a better word than 'fling' or 'affair.'"

"Definitely." He kissed her again, but then she forced him back to business. She had lists to go over with him, contacts and phone numbers for those she'd already contacted regarding the VIP dinner. Then she handed him the folder. "Promise me I won't hear another word about this dinner until the night of the event. Then, I'll be there with bells on to serve food or wait tables or pour wine."

"That's a deal." Which meant he would be the one coordinating with Melanie. That was okay—his cousins had softened toward him a lot. And the less time Melanie spent with Loretta, the less chance she would get to spill the beans about his past.

"MAMA, GUESS WHAT? *Tante* Celeste bought me an ice-cream cone."

Loretta was in her mother's kitchen getting things

started for their regular Sunday family dinner together when Zara burst in, breathless with excitement.

"*Tante* Celeste?"

"She told me to call her that. She said she has a granddaughter named Sylvie who's an artist and has red hair, just like me, and that I'm like she was when she was younger."

"That's very sweet of her."

Zara's gaze hadn't stopped darting around since she'd walked in the door. "Where's Luc?"

"He had to go home. He has guests to take care of at the B and B. But I told him either Grandma or I would take Mrs. Robichaux home."

"You don't have to. Miss Marjo took her. They got all excited talking about the opera house."

Well. Celeste was winning fans right and left. "Where's Grandma?"

"She went to find Granddaddy, I think. What's for dinner?"

"Roast beef with mashed potatoes." She put Zara to work making a salad, but Loretta's hands shook. Had Celeste gossiped about her and Luc? She had no reason to think her parents would disapprove. In fact, they often reminded her that she was still a very young woman and urged her to get out more and socialize. They both seemed to like Luc.

Still, it was unnerving. They'd been so disapproving of Jim, and so hurt when she'd run off and married him without their blessing. So dating was kind of a sore subject, for her, at least. Anyway, she'd wanted to be the one to tell them she was seeing Luc—and to do it without Zara around.

She would tell Zara tomorrow, when Luc came to their house to pick Loretta up for their first official date.

When her parents returned from tending the bees, she watched them closely to see if they knew anything, but they seemed perfectly normal.

She waited until after dessert, when she sent Zara to watch TV. "Don't I have to help clean the kitchen?" she asked, puzzled.

"Not tonight. You can have the night off."

Zara didn't question her good fortune and dashed into the den. Vincent tried to wander off himself, but Loretta called him back.

"I have something to tell you all," she announced.

Her mother put a hand to her mouth. "Oh, my God, you're pregnant."

"Mama! No." At least that little matter had been laid to rest. As of a couple of days ago, she was sure she wasn't pregnant. "But Luc and I are seeing each other."

"Oh."

"Is that your big news?" Vincent asked. "We knew that was coming. Saw it a mile off. "

"You could have clued me in."

"Everyone in town knew."

"What? Since when?"

"I dunno," Vincent said, glancing at the newspaper.

"Any fool could see you two are besotted with one another," Adele said. "Even before we talked about Luc the other day, I knew. About a month ago, we ran into him at the grocery store, remember? And your face got all pink, and you two talked about which fruits were in season. I knew then."

Loretta remembered the incident well. She'd been tongue-tied, which was unusual, and later she realized it was because her mother was right there, and she was embarrassed by the surge of inappropriate sexual longing that had descended on her in front of the blueberries.

"I wish you'd told me," Loretta said.

"Well, I'm glad it's official. Zara told me a couple of weeks ago she thought Luc was going to be her new daddy."

"Ah, Zara. I had to straighten things out with her. Luc and I aren't that serious. I mean, we're taking things one day at a time. Luc's a bit commitment-shy and, frankly, I'm not sure I ever want to get married again."

"Oh, Loretta." Adele said it the way she might if Loretta had just announced she had a fatal disease.

"Seriously. Zara had Luc and I married off when we'd never even held hands. I had to disabuse her of those notions. So don't go putting any ideas in her head, okay?"

"Who, us?" Vincent said as he put away the dishes Loretta was drying by hand. Her mother had a perfectly good dishwasher but for some unknown reason didn't like to use it.

Adele turned off the water and dried her hands. "But why wouldn't you want to marry someone as nice as Luc?"

"For one thing, he has no plans to stay in Indigo. Once the B and B renovation is complete, he's leaving. And I'm not."

"Oh. I see. Well, I'd rather you didn't move away. But sometimes a woman has to follow her man."

Loretta was shocked. "That's not what you said about Jim."

"Jim was an itinerant sharecropper without a dime to his name and he had shifty eyes," Adele explained. "I didn't want you going anywhere with him—or staying here with him, for that matter. Luc is an entirely different matter. Besides, you're grown up now. Yes, I want you and Zara close by. But I also want to see you happy."

"I am happy, Mama. I have wonderful parents, a wonderful daughter, a business I love. If I could have a man, too, that'd be great, but it's not a necessity."

"Hmm," her father said.

"What?"

"Nothing."

"I'D LIKE TO SEE my new boat, please."

Luc had been dreading this moment since Celeste's arrival two days earlier. She'd initially loved the idea of offering cruises to the B and B guests, but she'd become downright balky when it came to forking over the dough to buy a boat.

But Luc had talked her into it, confident he had plenty of time to refurbish the grimy pontoon boat he'd found before she saw it.

All he'd done so far was hose off several years of ac-cumulated swamp scum. He still needed to replace the cushions and canopy. It was, however, seaworthy, and the engine was in perfect running order.

But Celeste wouldn't focus on that.

"Good morning, *Grand-mère*," Luc said with faux cheerfulness, as he continued to beat the eggs for the omelets he had planned. With only two guests in residence, plus Celeste, he could afford to get fancy. He was going to customize each omelet, cooking it to order. "I can show you the boat right after breakfast." He saw no other choice; it was her boat.

"Very good," she said. "Now then, for breakfast, I'd like one plain croissant with butter and strawberry jam and two slices of lean, crisp bacon. Also some hot, decaffeinated tea with honey."

A plain croissant. It figured Celeste would ask for the one thing Loretta hadn't delivered earlier that morning. "How about a chocolate croissant? Or an almond one?"

She looked scandalized. "Why would anyone want to ruin a perfectly good, traditional French pastry with a lot of sugar and other nonsense?"

He took it that meant no. "I'm sorry, *Grand-mère,* I don't have any plain croissants. I have white, wheat, rye and pumpernickel bread, cranberry orange muffins, low-fat blueberry muffins, coffee cake—"

"What is the point of sleeping with a baker if she doesn't provide you with the correct breads?"

Luc gritted his teeth. His grandmother had made a career of provoking people. Sometimes he thought she was testing him to see how far she could push him before he blew—before he proved he was his father's son, lost his temper and walked out on her and her bed-and-breakfast. At which point she could have him arrested and force him to serve the remainder of his sentence behind bars.

He wouldn't play her game; he wouldn't give her the satisfaction.

"I'm not merely sleeping with Loretta," he said, keeping his voice even. "She's a very special person to me. I have a great deal of admiration and respect for her. But since I am not psychic, I didn't know that you would require a plain croissant this morning. So would you like one of the other choices? I can manage the bacon and the tea and all the rest."

He could have sworn the right corner of Celeste's mouth turned up, just slightly. So she was playing him for her own amusement.

"I'll just have what everyone else is having," she said. "And coffee is fine, never mind the tea. I'm used to having whatever I want at the Hotel Marchand when I visit, and I forget that a bed-and-breakfast is set up differently. Is there a newspaper I might read while I'm waiting?"

He softened slightly. Maybe he was judging her too harshly. "In the dining room. There are three different ones." He was almost afraid to offer her the omelet choices. Although he had nine different fillings on hand, she was sure to want something unavailable—anchovies or truffles.

A few minutes later, however, he was pleasantly surprised. His guests raved about the omelets, and Celeste ate a cinnamon roll *and* a chocolate croissant, obviously enjoying them. The couple from Mobile lured Celeste into conversation about some mutual acquaintances.

When the table was cleared and the dishwasher

loaded, Doc tapped on the kitchen door and leaned his head in. "Anyone home?"

"Hey, Doc," Luc greeted him, "come on in. What brings you around so early?" Doc usually saw patients in the morning on Mondays and Wednesdays—it was as close to retired as he'd been able to get.

"Oh, just out for my morning constitutional. Thought I'd stop by—oh, hello, Celeste. I didn't think you would be up so early."

"Early? It's almost nine o'clock."

Doc laughed at her curt tone as he poured himself a cup of coffee. "Why, I remember when you were a girl, your mama had a hard time prying you out of bed before noon!"

Celeste glared at Doc. "I don't think Luc is interested in my girlhood lack of discipline."

"On the contrary, *Grand-mère,* I find the details about your past very interesting, especially after seeing all those old pictures you brought."

Doc grinned, obviously enjoying Celeste's discomfort, so Celeste did the only thing she could under the circumstances. She took control by changing the subject. "Luc was about to show me the boat he manipulated me into buying."

Doc's smile vanished. He'd seen the boat. He could predict Celeste's reaction as easily as Luc could.

"Manipulated?" Luc objected. "You were the one who wanted to do more to attract the music festival crowd to the B and B."

"I got caught up in your enthusiasm," she insisted. "Temporarily."

"A boat's a good idea," Doc interjected. "You wouldn't believe what people around here charge for a swamp tour. Everyone's all keen to see a gator, or an ivory-billed woodpecker."

Celeste stood and smoothed the front of her impeccably pressed beige trousers. "Well, let's go have a look at this barge, then. Does it run? Can we take it out on the water?"

"Of course it runs," Luc said. "I wouldn't buy a boat that doesn't run. If Doc will watch the B and B for a few minutes—"

"The B and B can take care of itself," Celeste said. "I want Doc to come with us."

Good. Celeste was usually on better behavior when non-family members were around.

Luc got the boat keys, then they all went out the kitchen door and around to a wide, red-brick path that meandered across the gently sloping lawn toward the bayou, the same area where he'd found Zara hunting crawfish the previous week. Bricks eventually gave way to a wooden boardwalk over the squishy ground, and then to the dock where the boat was tied.

"Michel, would you give me your arm, please?" Celeste said, her voice almost coquettish. "I'm not wearing proper shoes for boating."

"Of course, my dear."

Luc resisted the urge to turn and stare at his grandmother. She was flirting with Doc! And Doc was flirting back. Luc shut his mind to the possibility. He refused to entertain the idea of his grandmother and Doc…what? Dating?

Did octogenarians do more than hold hands?

Luc squeezed his eyes shut and opened them again. "Well, here she is." He fervently wished he'd parked the boat nose-in the last time he'd taken it out, but he'd backed it up instead. A few leaves had collected on the faded green-and-white canopy, which was folded down for storage, but otherwise the boat didn't look as bad as he'd thought.

It was the boat's name, though, that caused him to wince.

Celeste studied the vessel from stem to stern with a keen eye. "Well, now, it doesn't look so bad. It's got good lines."

"I thought so," Luc said. As a child he'd been interested in boats and had studied pictures and read about them. He'd also worked a huge marine trade show in Las Vegas every year for three years before he'd left home. When he'd lived in Thailand he'd gotten out on the water every chance he had, so he knew a bit about watercraft.

"Let's see what she can—" Celeste stopped midsentence. "Oh. *Mon Dieu,* does that say…?" She was staring at the back of the boat. She'd seen it, the name.

"That's what it says, all right," Doc said. *"Bitchin' Mama."*

CHAPTER TWELVE

"LUC, TELL ME you didn't christen this boat the *Bitchin' Mama.*"

"No, it came like that," Luc quickly reassured her. "Don't worry, I'll change it."

"That should have been the first thing you did! Have you actually taken our guests out in this thing?"

Luc kicked a leaf off the dock. "I explained to them the circumstances."

"Couldn't you ink out the name with a Magic Marker? Cover it with duct tape? It's...it's an abomination."

"I'll scrape off the decal as soon as I can."

"Today."

"I have other work to do, *Grand-mère.* The B and B doesn't run itself. I have cleaning, laundry, grocery shopping—"

"You've become quite domestic since you moved to Indigo, haven't you."

"That's what you sent me here for, isn't it?"

"I wasn't complaining. Just that I think it's interesting."

So now he'd become her lab experiment. "I will try

to work on the boat sometime this week, but I can't today," he said firmly. Aside from having to clean up after a full house over the weekend, he'd promised Loretta he'd make some phone calls for the VIP dinner.

And then he had a date with Loretta. Or, more accurately, with Loretta and Zara. Tonight was the night they were sitting down with Zara to explain the nature of their relationship. And when they'd done that, he was taking Loretta out to dinner—a fancy, romantic dinner complete with candles and wine and soft music. He'd found a historic hotel in St. Martinville that fit the bill. She'd promised to arrange for a sitter for Zara— probably Adele and Vincent.

This would be Luc's first official date with Loretta. Maybe they'd gotten things a little backward, making love first, but no law said he couldn't set things right now.

Celeste looked as if she wanted to argue, but Doc stepped in. "Now, Celeste, let the boy alone. He's been running La Petite Maison just fine without anyone's help for several months now, and doing a fine job of it, too. You can't come roaring in here changing the order of things on a whim."

"Wanting *that* name off *my* boat is not a whim," she insisted mulishly.

"Why don't you take a spin in her?" Doc cajoled. "The smell of the bayou, the Spanish moss, trailing your hand in the water…remember how you used to do that?"

"Until an alligator almost took my arm off," she shot back, then laughed unexpectedly. "Oh, Michel, why don't you and I go for a ride? We'll just let Luc get back to his work."

Doc looked at Luc. "I can take your grandmother for a test drive. And I'll make her wear a life jacket."

Luc nodded and handed the keys to Doc, then leaned in and whispered, "Keep her out as long as you like. She doesn't have a curfew."

Doc roared with laughter and Celeste glowered. She didn't like anyone keeping secrets from her. But then she smiled and tilted her head at Doc. "Let's see what the *Bitchin' Mama* can do."

Luc laughed all the way back to the house.

LUC DIDN'T HAVE a lot of belongings he could call his own. Moving around most of his adult life, he simply hadn't accumulated much. But he did own a couple of good-quality suits and everything that went with them.

That afternoon, he washed his car, walked down to the barbershop and got his hair cut, then came home, ironed his favorite navy suit, and put it on. He cut some colorful chrysanthemums from the garden and wrapped them in wet paper towels and a plastic bag.

Then he wandered out to the veranda. Doc had spent the entire day hanging out with Celeste. They'd come back from their lengthy boat ride looking windblown, with ruddy cheeks and sparkling eyes. Luc wondered what they'd been doing besides taking in the local flora and fauna, then he'd immediately censored the thought. He did not want to go there.

"I'm leaving for the evening," he said.

Doc whistled. "Whoever she is, she must be special."

"You know who she is, and you know she's special."

"Why, Luc," Celeste said, "I don't think I've ever seen you looking so handsome."

"Thank you, *Grand-mère*." He could have said the same for her—that he'd never seen her looking quite so pretty. He gave her a courtly bow, then left for Loretta's. He hadn't felt this excited about a date since…maybe never.

As he drove up to the bakery, he realized he didn't know where the front door to Loretta's house was. He couldn't remember seeing one. The sign on the door had been turned to Closed, and it was dark inside.

But then he saw movement through the glass, and Loretta appeared with an apologetic smile as she unlocked the door. "I should have told you to walk around back to the kitchen," she said. "When I remodeled, I took off the whole front of the house so I don't have a front door any— Oh, my God, you look fabulous."

They stared at each other for a few seconds. Luc knew he should say something, but all his words were stuck in his throat. Loretta looked amazing. She was wearing a black velvet dress that showed a lot of leg and a lot of cleavage, and had tamed her usual spikes to a softer look, letting her hair fall into short tousled waves. She stared at him uncertainly. "Is something wrong?"

"No. Oh, no, it's just that you're so gorgeous you struck me dumb."

"Oh, Luc," she said, fluffing her hair self-consciously. He saw that she'd polished her nails for him— a dark, dramatic purple. She would probably have to turn around and remove every bit of that polish before she could do tomorrow's baking. "I'm not very good at this fancy-dress stuff, really. You look like you were born to it."

"I know how to clean up," he said with a grin. "Where's Zara?"

"I just sat her down with dinner. Are you ready for that talk?"

"Absolutely. Let's do it."

They moved from the dark bakery into the kitchen. Zara glanced up from her dinner of macaroni-and-cheese and broccoli, and her face lit up with pleasure.

"Luc."

"Hi, gorgeous."

"Mama said you're taking her out on a date." It was almost an accusation.

"Yes, that's right, I am."

Loretta pulled out a chair at the oak kitchen table and sat down, and Luc took that as his signal to do the same. "I know we both told you that we weren't dating, but as it turns out, we've changed our minds."

Zara looked down at her broccoli. "Okay."

Luc had thought she might be a bit more enthusiastic, that she'd be ready to send out the wedding invitations. Her cautious acceptance of the news seemed out of character. But maybe, after her last disappointment, she was afraid to hope for too much.

"We decided we like each other too much to be just friends," Luc added, though he was treading deep water here. "But we don't want to mislead you. We're not making any definite plans for the future."

"We're taking things one day at a time," Loretta added. "There's a very good chance Luc will be moving away from Indigo in a few months, so it doesn't make sense for us to make plans—you know, for a future. Long-term."

Loretta looked at Luc. He shrugged. He didn't know how to explain it any better than she just had.

"So Luc can't be my dad, ever," Zara said, trying to sound adult and practical. But her voice wavered, making Luc's chest hurt.

"Zara, if ever I was going to be a dad, I'd want a little girl just like you. No, let me say it stronger. I'd want you. But—"

"I know, you can't make promises."

"If you want to do some things together, just you and me, we can," he said. "And we can all do things together, you and your mom and me. We can have a lot of fun. And later, if I do go away, we'll have great memories."

"I still don't know why you want to go away," Zara said.

"Maybe I won't. Maybe I'll stay longer." It was the first time he'd acknowledged, out loud, that he might stick around, and it surprised even him. "The point is, we don't know right now what the future will bring. But we want to enjoy the time together we do have and not worry so much about what's coming. Can you understand that?"

She nodded. "I think so."

"Then could we have a smile?" Luc asked. "Let's not be sad till we have a reason to be sad."

Zara smiled. It was forced at first, but then seemed to grow until it was real.

"I'll let you two visit while I finish getting ready," Loretta said. "Zara, hurry and finish your dinner. You're going to spend the night at Grandma and Granddaddy's tonight."

"On a school night?"

"Uh-huh. And I've told your grandma to let you stay up a half hour later so you can watch that doctor show you like. Since Luc is giving me a special treat tonight, I thought it was only fair you should get one, too."

"Yay!" Zara dug into her macaroni with renewed vigor. She was lucky to have such a good relationship with her grandparents, Luc thought. His maternal grandparents had lived in Trenton, New Jersey, and Luc had met them only a couple of times before his grandmother had died and his grandfather had gone into a nursing home, where he'd died a short time later. And of course, he'd never met Celeste until a couple of years ago when he'd gone to work for the Hotel Marchand.

His mother would have liked grandchildren to dote on. But since he was her only child, it didn't seem likely she would get any. Maybe he could take Loretta and Zara to Vegas sometime to meet his mother. She would enjoy fussing over Zara.

But immediately he realized how impossible that was. So long as there was no commitment between himself and Loretta, he would only be setting up more false expectations.

"Luc, do you know how to fish?" Zara asked.

"Actually, no." Despite his affinity for boats, fishing was something he'd never tried. "Do you want to teach me how?"

"I don't know how, either. Except for catching crawdads."

"Maybe that's something we can learn together. I have a boat, and the bayou is right outside my back door. Seems like it shouldn't be that hard."

"My friend Kiki's mother's boyfriend took her fishing on Lake Pontchartrain. Just her and him."

"Does that sound like something you want to do?"
She nodded.

"Then we'll do it. I'll make it happen."

"When?"

"How about the weekend after the music festival."

She sighed. "That's forever away."

"I know, but things are a little crazy until it's over. Your mom needs my help. And I'm not sure how my grandmother will feel about me taking an afternoon off to go fishing."

"I like *Tante* Celeste. Maybe she could go with us."

Oh, now, *that* he would like to see—Celeste baiting a fishhook with a worm. The mental image made him laugh. "I'll ask her."

A few minutes later, Luc and Loretta dropped off Zara at her grandparents' house. Then they drove the five or so miles to St. Martinville. Luc wished he had one of those old cars with bench seats, so Loretta could snuggle up next to him. He settled for reaching over to hold her hand.

"How do you think we did with Zara?"

"Mmm, hard to tell. She keeps her cards close to her chest. But we did the best we could."

"I promised to take her fishing. I hope that's okay."

"Fishing! That's strange."

"Kiki's mother's boyfriend took Kiki fishing."

"Ah. I get it. Well, at least now we don't have to hide anything. I don't like keeping secrets from Zara—or from anyone, really. I'm not a good liar."

"Speaking of keeping secrets, did you know there was something going on between Celeste and Doc?"

"I thought there might be. How lovely. Do you think it's serious?"

"I don't know. It's just so…weird."

"Because they're senior citizens?"

"No, because she's my grandmother. And because she's Celeste. You don't know her like I do. She's usually all proper and snooty and looking down her nose at everyone. Now here she is, giggling like a schoolgirl and…and flirting."

"Maybe she's in love. Or moving that way. Love can be very transformative, you know."

"So I hear." Watching all his cousins fall in love when he'd been working at the hotel was one of the reasons he'd come to like them so much. He'd seen every side of them—seen them angry, vulnerable, hurting and ultimately very happy.

"Yes, love can make a huge difference in a person's life. But it can also be destructive." Like his father's careless love for his mother. He'd given her just enough love to make her long for more—just enough to keep her from divorcing him, at least during those first few years.

"But how could it ever work out for them?" Loretta

asked. "Doc has lived in Indigo his whole life. He would never move to New Orleans."

Luc was silent for a few moments as he thought about that. Then, he got it. Of *course* Celeste had a master plan. She hadn't given him the task of renovating the cabin simply out of kindness or compassion for him, or guilt that perhaps she owed her dead son something. She'd had her own selfish reasons.

"Oh, my God. She's going to move to Indigo."

"You think?"

"It all fits! She had me renovate the cabin so she'd have a place to live. Now she's going to watch how I run the bed-and-breakfast so she can do it herself—or hire someone else. The whole opera house/museum thing—she's trying to ingratiate herself into the fabric of Indigo society so that when she moves here, she'll already be an insider."

"So you think she's here to stay?"

What a scary thought. "I can't live in that house with my grandmother for six months."

"Six months? Luc, is there a timetable I'm not aware of?"

Yeah, the remainder of his probation. "I'd always planned on staying here two years," he said carefully, not wanting to lie outright. "Next April will be two years."

"You could always move in with me and Zara."

The invitation hung in the air and an awkward silence filled the car.

"Sorry, scratch that," Loretta said with a nervous laugh. "That was probably a bit premature. Considering this is our first date."

But he couldn't forget she'd said it. The fact she would even consider it, after he'd given her fair warning that he wasn't the sticking-around kind, was amazing. But the really scary part was how attractive the prospect was to him.

If he moved in with Loretta and Zara, he might never want to leave.

Of course, it was all conjecture, anyway. He had to stay at the B and B and run it for the term of his probation—no way out of that, Celeste or no Celeste.

THEIR ROMANTIC DINNER was everything Luc had hoped it would be. They put aside all discussion of anything more serious than the merits of the wine and food. They lingered over dessert, and afterward took a walk around the historic downtown area, holding hands and whispering to each other like besotted lovers.

When he took her home, they made love, and for the first time it was slow, leisurely—and in the dark. Luc found that darkness added a whole new dimension to the experience, allowing his other senses to become heightened. He could focus for minutes at a time on the exquisite texture of Loretta's skin, the smell of her hair, the way her soft sighs reverberated along his nerve endings.

It was less sex than it was worship. And when she finally pleaded for him to leave so she could at least get a couple of hours' sleep before she had to get up and bake, he did so with a smile on his face. Even with all of the future's uncertainties, he felt happier than he could ever remember feeling, like there was a balloon inside his chest. But he couldn't escape the niggling sensation that someone, somewhere, was standing by with a sharp pin.

LORETTA AWOKE with her alarm at four. Though she'd had less than three hours' sleep, she had no trouble bouncing out of bed and into the shower. Her "first date" with Luc had gone pretty well, all things considered.

She'd made a couple of serious gaffes. The first had been to talk about love. Guys sometimes ran for the hills at the mere mention of the L-word, even in casual conversation. At least, that's what she'd heard. She had no practical experience, because Jim had declared himself in love with her less than a week after meeting her. Still, she'd known better than to tread on that dangerous ground when her relationship with Luc was so tenuous.

His response—that love could be destructive—could have sent the evening on a downhill spiral. But somehow they'd salvaged it.

Then she'd made an even worse mistake by inviting him to move in with her. She had no idea where that had come from. The words had bypassed her brain completely. But the thought that his grandmother's machinations might drive him away from Indigo earlier than anticipated had panicked her. She'd resigned herself to the fact that happily-ever-after was not even a remote possibility for herself and Luc, but she'd been counting on having him around at least a few months.

The thought of losing any of that time…well, she'd

just spoken without thinking. At least she'd had the sense to withdraw the offer and laugh at herself, no matter how much she'd been shriveling inside.

Amazingly, she hadn't ruined the evening. And her sense of optimism about the future hadn't dimmed, no matter what reality dictated. She felt fantastic.

Everything she baked that morning turned out better than perfect—a little puffier, a little sweeter, as if her good mood had infused the dough with a pinch of magic. She included three extra cranberry muffins in Luc's order.

He greeted her at the back door with a sleepy smile. And when she handed him his basket full of goodies, exchanging it for an empty one, he grabbed her and kissed her and threatened not to let her make the rest of her deliveries.

"I have to go," she said for the third time.

"Come back when you're done," he said.

"Luc, I have a business to run. If I keep closing the bakery every time I want to see you—well, it might just stay closed."

"Stop for ten minutes. Long enough for a cup of coffee. I need my Loretta fix."

"Last night wasn't enough?"

"Not near enough. A hundred last nights wouldn't be enough."

She stopped herself before she asked him just how many *would* be enough. That was her insecurity talking, and she had to banish those thoughts if she wanted this one-day-at-a-time plan to be a success.

"Ten minutes—for coffee," she said, making sure he understood and would not tempt her.

After her rounds, she dropped off free samples to three more prospective customers. She had learned that samples worked better than any other advertising she could do. Then she headed for the B and B, her heart fluttering ridiculously at the prospect of seeing Luc, even if it were for only ten minutes.

She was crazy. Or maybe she was in love. The symptoms seemed right. She wouldn't have chosen to fall for Luc Carter, knowing the eventual outcome would be painful. But there wasn't much she could do about it except go with the flow. Enjoy it while she could. Following Luc's advice to Zara last night, she refused to be sad until she had a reason to be sad.

He was watching for her as she approached the pretty cottage.

"I missed you," he said the moment he opened the door.

"You saw me a couple of hours ago."

"I know. Just tell me to shut up. I'm getting a little crazy."

"If you're crazy, I'm crazy, too."

He kissed her, then poured her the coffee he'd promised. They'd just settled at the kitchen table when the front bell rang.

"You expecting anyone?" Loretta asked.

"No, but maybe it's a walk-in. The billboard I put up on the main highway has brought quite a few people in."

Loretta followed him to the door. She enjoyed watching him deal with the public, and her time with him this morning was limited, so she didn't want to waste any of it sitting alone in the kitchen.

Luc opened the door to admit a lone man, mid-twenties, in a brown suit and well-worn shoes. He did not look like your typical B and B customer.

"Hello, are you Luc Carter?"

"Yes," Luc answered warily. "Can I help you?"

"I'm Isaac Belton."

Luc looked at him blankly.

"I think you must have gotten a letter from the state, advising you that I'd be taking over the duties of your former probation officer, since he's been transferred to New Orleans."

Loretta's coffee mug slipped through her fingers and landed with a crash on the cypress floor. Both men looked over at her, startled.

"Loretta—" Luc said, but he stopped there. What could he say, she wondered, to soften the shock of what she'd just learned? Nothing. There was absolutely nothing he could say.

And there was nothing she wanted to say. Bad manners though it was, she turned and fled without a word, without cleaning up the mess or apologizing for breaking Luc's mug. She could think of nothing but escape.

CHAPTER THIRTEEN

"LORETTA! Wait a minute!" Luc ran after her, but she was already behind the wheel of her car by the time he reached the driveway. He knocked on her window, but she wouldn't even look at him. She cranked the engine and backed out, spraying gravel, completely oblivious to him. She'd have backed over his foot if he hadn't jumped out of the way.

He watched her go, feeling a sense of loss and desolation so great he couldn't find words to describe it.

His visitor followed him out into the driveway. "Did I say something wrong?"

"You didn't have to say anything. Just showing up was enough."

"Girlfriend?" the probation officer asked.

"Ex-girlfriend now, would be my guess."

"She didn't know of your…situation?"

Luc shook his head. "I was going to tell her. But I hadn't gotten around to it. I never imagined you would show up here. Mr. Conley never did."

"Which was one reason he was transferred. He was a little, shall we say, lax? Making unannounced visits to a client's home or place of business is standard operating procedure."

"I don't have a problem with that. Your timing sucks, that's all."

"I'm sorry," the man said, sounding sincere. "It's not my aim to cause problems for you. I want you to adjust, and part of that adjustment is to form bonds within a support network that will—"

"Yeah, I know," Luc said woodenly. "That was exactly what I was doing. I was finally starting to feel like a part of the town, a member of the community. But once it gets all over that I'm a convicted felon—"

"I understand. I guess I didn't realize the repercussions an unannounced visit could have. I'm, uh, new at this."

Luc could have made the guy feel worse, but what was the point? The damage was done. "Come on inside, have some coffee. I'll show you what I've been doing with myself for the past umpteen months."

Thankfully none of the guests were around. But Celeste made an appearance just as Isaac Belton was finishing up with his questions. She'd slept in that morning, for the first time since she'd arrived in Indigo.

Luc groaned inwardly, not too keen for his grandmother to meet his new probation officer.

"Good morning, Luc," she said as she headed for the coffee pot. "I apologize for missing breakfast, but I feel like I might be coming down with a cold, so I thought getting some extra rest would be helpful. Good morning," she said to Mr. Belton, probably thinking he was a new B and B guest.

Luc privately thought his grandmother's sleeping late had nothing to do with any cold. He'd heard someone tiptoeing down the squeaky wood stairs last night at an ungodly hour and leaving by the kitchen door. The most likely candidate was Doc, though Luc hadn't cared to confirm his suspicions. He'd put his pillow over his head and hoped to forget the incident by morning.

"I'll fix you something for breakfast, *Grand-mère,* in just a few minutes."

"Oh, so this is your grandmother," Isaac Belton said. "The one who owns La Petite Maison?"

"Yes, that's right," Celeste said. "Celeste Robichaux." And she extended her hand like a duchess expecting an underling to kiss her ring.

The probation officer took her hand and gave it a squeeze. "I'm Isaac Belton, your grandson's new—" He stopped and looked at Luc, as if to seek permission.

Luc just shrugged and nodded. It couldn't get much worse, unless Celeste told this guy she'd seen Luc doing drugs or stealing jewelry from his guests.

"I'm a probation officer from New Iberia," Mr. Belton said. "I've recently taken over Luc's file, and I came here to introduce myself. I was also frankly curious about this place. I own a similar type of house, only it hasn't been renovated. Your B and B is an inspiration to me."

"It's all Luc's doing," Celeste said. "I had the idea to turn it into a B and B, but Luc did every bit of the renovations, the décor, the advertising and marketing, everything. He even cooks! I couldn't have put this place into better hands." She gave Luc a wink behind the probation officer's back, acknowledging that she was laying it on a little thick.

"I can see that," Mr. Belton said. He made a notation in his notebook. "I've seen everything I need to see, Luc, so I'll leave you to your work. See you next Tuesday at my office?"

As if Luc had a choice. "Yes, sir."

"And I am sorry about my lack of tact earlier. I'd be happy to talk to your friend if you think it would help."

"No, thanks." Luc couldn't imagine anything that *would* help. Loretta's worst nightmare had come to pass—she'd become involved with another criminal. Worse, she'd let her impressionable daughter associate with a felon. If he'd been able to tell her about his past in his own way, in his own time, maybe he'd have stood a chance of not driving her off. But now...

Ah, hell. By not telling Loretta the truth, he'd only delayed the inevitable.

"Well, good day, then." Mr. Belton tipped an imaginary hat, one of those impossibly gallant Southern-gentleman gestures. "Mrs. Robichaux, enjoy your visit."

Luc walked him to the front door. After he'd closed it, he turned to find Celeste standing right behind him. "Thank you, *Grand-mère,* for saying those nice things." He meant it. The woman wielded a lot of power over him, and she knew how to use it. A few well-placed words in the wrong ear, and he could end up wearing prison stripes.

"You're family, Luc," she said, her voice warmer than he'd ever heard it. "We have to stick up for each other. Perhaps if I'd been a little more understanding and forgiving with your father, things would have turned out differently."

Luc was so shocked, he couldn't respond. First, that his grandmother actually considered him family. And second, that she was admitting she might have been wrong, at least partly. That wasn't her usual M.O.

"What did Mr. Belton mean when he said he was sorry about his lack of tact?"

Luc grimaced. "He spilled the beans to Loretta."

"She didn't take the news well?"

"To put it mildly."

Celeste shook her head. "I'm sorry to hear that. I like Loretta. But maybe it's good the truth is out."

Celeste wouldn't say that if she'd seen the way Loretta had torn out of there a few minutes earlier.

"Do you want me to talk to her?" Celeste asked.

"Thank you, *Grand-mère,* but no. I'll talk to her once she settles down." In about a million years.

LORETTA HAD NO IDEA how she made it home without driving into a ditch or hitting a stop sign, her eyes blurry with tears. Still, she managed to blank her mind until she was safely parked at the side of the bakery. Then she ran for the front door, fumbled with the keys and finally unlocked the door.

Fortunately there were no walk-in customers waiting for her to open. She made her way through the darkened bakery and into her house. She didn't stop until she reached the safety of her bedroom, where she flopped on her bed like a melodramatic teenager and gave full vent to her emotions.

She wasn't so much sad as furious—and when she was angry, she cried. Luc had a probation officer! All this time she'd thought he was hardworking, honest and generous, when he was actually a criminal.

What was wrong with her? The only two men she'd ever been strongly attracted to were criminals. Did she have some self-destructive streak?

And Zara! She'd had to accept that her father was a criminal, and now Luc.

They didn't give guys with too many traffic tickets a probation officer. Luc must have done something awful, something unspeakable. How had he fooled her? Why had she trusted him?

Loretta beat and twisted one of her feather pillows until it was an unrecognizable knot. Luc hadn't fooled just her. He'd taken in the whole town with his good-guy act, ingratiating himself into the community, volunteering to help with the music festival. Didn't he have an obligation to tell them what he really was?

Her instincts had warned her to stay away from him, with his easy charm and his mysterious past. She should have listened to them.

Disillusioned, Loretta gave herself an hour to mourn the loss of her short-lived romance. Then she got up, pulled herself together, washed her face and put some gel in her hair, spiking it severely, telling the world to go to hell. She had to open the bakery before someone noticed she'd been closed for an extended period and started to worry about her.

She looked awful. Her nose was red and her eyes puffy. But at least she was done crying for the moment. She fixed herself a cup of hot tea and warmed up one of her favorite, butter-laden cinnamon rolls. Then she tackled her list of tasks for the music festival.

Every person she talked to asked if something was wrong, even people who didn't know her. She claimed she was coming down with a cold to explain her stuffy nose and scratchy-sounding voice.

At three o'clock she realized she had orders for Zara's schoolmates to package, and the bus would be around in half an hour. She zoomed around the bakery and managed to pull everything together just in time.

Della Roy stepped down from behind the wheel of her bus and handed Loretta five checks and a bundle of cash, trading the payments for six labeled bakery bags. "Loretta, you look awful," she said. "I mean, gorgeous as always, but kind of puffy."

"Cold," Loretta mumbled.

Zara tumbled off the bus, studying her mother carefully. "Mama, you do look funny."

"I know, sweetie. Thank you, Della. I included some snickerdoodles this time. Let me know if you like them."

"Will do. Take care of yourself."

The bus pulled away, and Zara took Loretta's hand as they walked back to the bakery. She asked for a snack, and Loretta silently cut up an apple.

"Mama, what's wrong?"

Loretta pinched the bridge of her nose with her thumb and forefinger. Yet another horror—breaking the news to Zara that they would not have anything further to do with Luc Carter.

Although she didn't believe in lying to children, she didn't have the fortitude right now to deal with her daughter's questions, which she would surely have when she learned the new state of things. "I told you, I'm not feeling well."

"Did you take some medicine?"

"I'll be fine, honey. Don't worry."

"You could go see Doc. He could give you a shot."

Doc no doubt knew everything that was going on with Luc. He'd been spending time at the B and B almost every day since it opened. And yet he'd allowed Luc to hang out with Loretta and Zara, knowing their history.

Loretta had known Doc her whole life and thought he had better judgment than that. Then again, maybe Luc had fooled Doc, too. He was very good.

"I'm fine, Zara," she assured her daughter again. "You don't have to worry about me. I'm the mom, you're the little girl. I get to worry. You don't have to."

"I can't help it."

She sighed, set Zara's snack down and joined her at the table. "I know, sweetie. You're a very caring and concerned person, and that's good. But you'll have plenty of chances to worry when you grow up. I just want you to enjoy being a little girl."

"I'd rather be a grown-up," she said candidly. "Then no one could tell me what to do."

"I'll tell you a secret," Loretta said. "Sometimes, when you're grown up, you wish someone *would* tell you what to do." If some wise person had been looking after Loretta's interests, maybe they would have told her to be more careful when it came to giving her heart away.

Her heart. No, it wasn't that serious. She'd made love with Luc three times and gone out with him once, not counting the trip to New Orleans. She hadn't had a chance to actually give him her heart. It was all physical at this point; it shouldn't be that big a deal to walk away now.

But it was. She had to face the fact it was going to be hard as hell to get over this. She would have a difficult time ever trusting herself when it came to men. Maybe she was meant to be alone.

"My birthday's coming up," Zara said.

Thank God, a nice, safe topic of conversation. "That's right, it's less than a month away." Loretta had been so fixated on the music festival—and Luc—that she hadn't given Zara's birthday a single thought. "Do you have any idea what you might like?"

"I have lots of ideas, but I think I want a fishing pole."

"A fishing pole?" What happened to dolls, and stuffed animals, and all that girlie stuff Zara usually drooled over whenever they went to a toy store?

"For when I go fishing with Luc."

"You're not going fishing with Luc." The words were out of Loretta's mouth, sharp and final, before she had a chance to soften them.

Zara's eyes widened. "But you said—"

"I've changed my mind. We really don't know Luc well enough for you to go fishing with him."

"But Kiki goes—"

"I don't care what Kiki does."

She expected Zara to run crying from the bakery,

which was her usual reaction on those rare occasions when Loretta was sharp with her or denied her something she wanted badly. Instead, she studied her mother with unnerving intensity.

"You're not being fair."

"Life isn't fair. And the sooner you learn that lesson, the better."

Zara pushed her plate away. "Did you and Luc have a fight?"

Oh, why did her daughter have to be so perceptive? "I can't talk about it, Zara. You're going to have to take my word for it for now—Luc Carter is out of our lives."

"Why?"

"You don't need to know why. Just accept it." No matter how angry she was with Luc and the secrets he'd kept from her, it wasn't her place to reveal that he was a criminal. She remembered how painful it was years ago when news of Jim's arrest for robbing a convenience store had spread all over town like wildfire.

Now Zara showed her temper. She pushed her chair back so hard she almost toppled it and stomped out of the bakery.

"Zara, take your backpack—"

But Zara ignored her. Loretta knew she shouldn't allow her daughter to show her temper and act disrespectfully, but she was in no mood to correct her. She was still raw with her own anger, and she would probably just make things worse if she tried to talk to Zara now.

Luc was going to be a sticky subject for weeks to

come—for Zara and for Loretta herself. Zara would bounce back, eventually. Loretta wasn't sure if she ever would.

CELESTE PUTTERED AROUND her family's old summer cottage, her mind awash with memories. She'd been a very different person as a young girl. Wealthy, very aware of her own beauty and the power and influence of her family, she'd enjoyed being the center of attention in her social circle.

A lot of young men had shown interest. The most passionate of them all, the one who'd challenged her the most, was Michel Landry. Although close to her own age, he'd seemed older somehow. More mature, more seasoned than so many of the boys she had dated. Perhaps it was the fact he hadn't come from a privileged background. He'd had to work for a living from the time he was sixteen. He'd also served overseas during World War II, a fate many of her class avoided through various strategies. His years in the service had given him a certain maturity.

He'd been in love with her, of that she was sure. But he'd also been very aware of the games she played—and he hadn't fallen for them. Despite his lack of social status, he hadn't kowtowed to her or indulged her every whim.

He'd stood up to her, making it very clear that if they were to end up together, she would not be pulling his strings. He'd also been pretty firm about the fact that, once he graduated from medical school, he wanted to open a practice in Indigo rather than New Orleans.

Although her family had liked Michel, Celeste's mother had advised her to marry a man of her own class, so that she could maintain her rightful station in New Orleans society. And Celeste herself had decided her life would be easier if she married a man she could control, instead of one who challenged her in every way.

It was a decision she'd regretted almost every day of her life, but especially recently as she'd watched her daughter and granddaughters fall in love and marry for love.

When she first got the idea to come to Indigo, she'd told herself it was solely to look after her family's property and see for herself what Luc was doing with it.

But deep down, she knew there was more to it. She and Michel had kept in touch over the years, even if it was only to exchange Christmas cards. He'd been hurt when she'd turned down his marriage proposal, but he'd never held her decision against her. And when she'd felt the need to keep tabs on Luc, Michel had been the one she'd turned to.

She'd been terrified to actually call him on the telephone, her heart racing as she punched in the numbers, just as it had done when she was a teenager. And then she'd heard his voice—rough with age, but still undeniably, unmistakably, Michel Landry, and the years had melted away.

She'd been shocked to discover he was widowed— for almost three years. She supposed that was when the idea had crept into her mind that the embers of their decades-old romance might be rekindled.

So now here she was, and Michel had been courting her with the ardency of the young man he'd once been. The years had dissolved as they'd enjoyed cocktails on the veranda every afternoon.

And then last night…oh, my. She'd had no idea she still had it in her.

But what to do now?

She reached into the bottom of the box she'd brought with her from New Orleans and pulled out a small, framed family photo. It wasn't one that was really appropriate for the display at the opera house because it was a bit blurry. But she'd always loved it.

It showed a group of young people enjoying drinks—probably mint juleps—on the veranda here at the house, circa the mid-1940s, just after the war. Michel had his arm around her waist, and she was laughing up at him. They looked so in love, it made her heart ache.

There were no such pictures of herself and Arnaud Robichaux.

She set the photo on the mantel, along with a couple of other family-oriented pictures. She didn't think Luc would mind, and she hoped Michel would notice it and remember how close they had once been. Although he'd clearly shown his interest in her recently, he hadn't said anything about love. Or the future.

At their age, they couldn't pussyfoot around. She had to make some decisions about her future—however long or short that might be.

When she heard the back door open, her heart fluttered like a silly thing. "Hallo, anyone home?"

Celeste resisted the urge to run to the kitchen, and focused on arranging the photographs. "I'm in the parlor, Michel." She still didn't turn to look when she heard his footsteps enter the room, though it was killing her.

"Luc's gone to the store in New Iberia to buy groceries, but he should be home soon."

"Luc's not who I came to see, *chère*. So stop playing coy and give me a proper greeting."

"Michel, really." She tried to sound disapproving, but a renegade giggle gave her away.

He reached her in three strides and swept her into his arms. "You can't fool me anymore, Celeste. You want the same thing I want." He kissed her with much more passion than an eighty-something-year-old man should be able to muster, and she answered with equal ardor, surprising herself yet again.

But did he want what she wanted? Did he think it was possible to make up for the mistakes she'd made as a young woman and start over? Or was she just an old fool?

She pulled away from him. "Michel. We have to talk."

"If you're going to tell me we're too old to mess around, I'm not listening."

"No, that isn't it."

At the uncertain tremor in her voice, Michel sobered and led her to the settee. He cupped her face gently in his hand. "What is it, love?" The endearment slipped out easily, and he didn't seem embarrassed by it.

Well, if he wasn't embarrassed by his feelings, then she wouldn't be, either. For once in her life, she would strike out boldly without being in control, without knowing how it was all going to turn out.

"Michel, how would you feel about my moving to Indigo?"

"For how long?"

"For the rest of my life."

There was a long pause. "You want to live here? I thought you loved New Orleans. The excitement of the big city, the theater and opera and ballet, the shopping and—"

"Those are things I loved as a young woman. But my priorities have changed. I…I was stupid and self-absorbed when I was young. I didn't know what I was doing. I made a terrible mistake by not marrying you when I had the chance, and I'm sorry. I'm so sorry I hurt you."

She was blurting it all out now, but she couldn't seem to stop herself.

Michel drew back, looking almost comically shocked. "Why, Celeste, I never thought I'd see the day you would admit you were wrong about anything."

"I'd ask you to stop teasing, but the sad thing is, I know you're serious. I've always thought I knew what was best for everyone. But how could that be true, when I didn't even know what was best for myself?"

"You think you do now?"

"Yes. You're the best thing for me, Michel. You bring out everything that's good in me. You don't let me get away with anything. I want to be with you."

For the first time, he looked uncomfortable. Oh, *Dieu,* was he going to turn her down? Was he going to tell her she was fine for a roll in the hay but he'd rather marry an alligator than her?

It was probably what she deserved.

Michel reached into his vest pocket and pulled something out, but he kept it hidden from view. It might have been a breath mint, or just about anything. "When you say you want to be *with* me…"

"I want to marry you, silly as that is. But I'd settle for living in sin."

"Celeste!"

"Oh, I don't care what people think anymore."

"You do and you know it."

"All right, I suppose I do. But I'm prepared to withstand the gossip."

"Let me get this straight. You want to move to Indigo. Permanently. And be my girl, married or not."

"That's about the size of it." It felt good, she realized, to be perfectly honest. No games, no manipulation, no withholding anything. If he laughed at her, at least she knew she'd tried her very best.

But he didn't laugh, and instead extended his hand and opened his fingers to reveal a lovely oval diamond ring. "Then you might be interested in this."

She was afraid to touch it, afraid she had misunderstood. It couldn't be this easy. She gave him a questioning look.

"I've been carrying it around in my pocket since the day you arrived in Indigo, trying to work up the courage to ask you to marry me. It's the one I bought in 1945, when I asked you to marry me the first time. I could have returned it to the jewelry store or sold it, but I never did."

"Oh, Michel. I don't know what to say."

He slid off the sofa onto one knee, wincing slightly. "This isn't as easy as it was the first time, at least not on my knees. Celeste, will you marry me?"

"Oh, get up, you fool. I already said I would." She pulled him to his feet, then wrapped her arms around him and wept on his shoulder. It was a good kind of crying, though.

Michel patted her on the back and smoothed her hair, and after a minute or two, Celeste pulled an embroidered handkerchief out of her sleeve and blotted her eyes, knowing she looked a mess.

"Shall we elope like a couple of teenagers?"

"I think that would be the best thing."

"Michel, I want to show you something." She led him back to the mantel and took the photograph down, the one of the two of them on the veranda. "Look at us."

"Oh, my, weren't we a dashing couple."

"And so in love. The way we're looking at each other…"

"Reminds me of the way Luc and Loretta look at each other," Michel said. "At first I was skeptical of those two getting together, but now I can see they're exactly right for each other."

"If they don't ruin things. Oh, Michel, it wouldn't be fair, us being so happy and the young people so miserable. We have to do something to help."

"I don't know that Loretta is going to soften," Michel considered, stroking his chin. "She has some mighty powerful reasons not to trust men in general and Luc in particular."

"I'll talk to her. I'll make her see that she can't turn her back on love if there's any chance to make it work."

CHAPTER FOURTEEN

"MELANIE, COME IN." Luc opened the door wider to admit his cousin, who'd come to Indigo to check out the facilities and the site of the banquet.

She looked around with wide eyes. "This place is incredible. I remember coming here once when I was a little girl. The whole house was trashed."

"It was pretty bad," Luc agreed. "But it was fun fixing it up."

"You didn't just fix it up, you transformed it." Melanie inspected the furniture, the pictures, the rugs. "You really have an eye for color. Where's *Grand-mère?*"

"She's out."

"Out? Out where?"

"I'm not sure. She doesn't give me her agenda."

"Luc, she's almost eighty-six years old. You can't just let her go gallivanting around the countryside by herself. What if she falls? What if she gets sick?"

"Like I have any say over what she does? When was the last time you tried to tell her she couldn't do something?"

"Good point. But aren't you worried?"

"She's not alone. She has a boyfriend."

Melanie's jaw dropped. "You're joking."

"Apparently they were in love way back when, before she married our grandfather. They've rekindled the flame."

"Luc, this is dangerous. What if he's a fortune hunter? Celeste has millions."

Luc shook his head. "He's not a fortune hunter. He's the town doctor, salt of the earth, and I believe he genuinely cares for Celeste."

Melanie gave him a suspicious look. "How do I know you didn't cook all this up? You could be in cahoots with this guy."

Luc thought he couldn't feel any worse than he did after Loretta dumped him, but Melanie's lack of faith made him feel sick inside. For the first time, he had to come face-to-face with the fact that he might never fully regain his family's trust.

"I don't blame you for thinking that," he said. "Celeste should be back in a little while. You can talk to her, and to Doc. Hell, talk to anyone in this town about Doc. It'll put your mind at ease."

Melanie looked down at her shoes. "I'm sorry, Luc. I don't know what made me say that. Celeste isn't feeble-minded, and she's never been a sucker. She believes in you, and she obviously believes in this Doc person, so I will, too."

She suddenly stepped forward and hugged Luc, and he couldn't have been more surprised. He squeezed her back. "Thanks, Melanie. Let me show you the kitchen, and then we can go look at the opera house. Celeste will probably be back by then."

"Has it been awful, having her here?" Melanie asked in a whisper, as if the walls might overhear and report back to Celeste. "I love Queen Cee, but I'd go crazy having her around all the time, looking over my shoulder, criticizing."

"You know, surprisingly, it hasn't been too bad. I think she's getting soft in her old age."

"You gotta be kidding."

Luc shrugged. "You'll see."

Melanie inspected Luc's kitchen like an army general inspecting the troops. He'd cleaned it until it sparkled this morning, so she wouldn't find anything wanting.

"You sprang for some decent appliances, I'll say that," she said appreciatively.

"Celeste did. She understood the need for professional grade. On weekends when I'm cooking breakfast for ten or twelve people, I'm grateful."

Melanie nodded approvingly and made a few notations in a small notebook.

"Let's go see the opera house. Didn't it used to be an antique store?"

"Until recently. The shop's owner, Maude Picard, passed away. Her goddaughter moved the business to a little storefront."

They made the short drive in Luc's Tahoe. Melanie admired the opera house's simplified Greek revival style and paused to read the tarnished brass plaque identifying the building as having been designed by a famous New Orleans architect, James Gallier Jr.

Marjo had said she would leave a key in the mailbox

for Luc, but the door was already open when they arrived, so they walked in.

"This is gorgeous," Melanie said, gawking at the opera house's faded elegance. "Imagine what it must have been like in its glory days."

"The city is hoping to see it like that again. If the festival is a success, it should draw a lot of musicians and music lovers. The idea is that the opera house will be a center for Cajun and zydeco music—sort of a mini-Grand Ole Opry for the region."

"I can definitely see that." After locating all the working electrical outlets, Melanie took out a tape measure and checked the dimensions of the lobby. "It'll be a tight fit, serving a sit-down dinner for fifty, but it's doable. Have you rented the tables and chairs?"

"And the linens, china, flatware and crystal. If people are paying fifty bucks a plate, I figure they shouldn't have to eat off paper plates."

"Excellent. You've thought of everything. How did you get to be so good at event planning?"

"Hanging out at hotels all my life. Watching and learning."

"If you ever need a job…" She stopped, realizing what she was about to say.

"Don't worry, I don't expect the family to employ me once my probation is up."

"Don't rule out the possibility."

Luc didn't believe in a million years that his Aunt Anne or Cousin Charlotte, kind as they were, would want him back at the Hotel Marchand. Not after what he'd done.

They heard laughter coming from up in the balconies and realized they weren't alone. Melanie's eyebrows flew up. "Is the opera house haunted?"

Luc grinned. "You don't recognize the laughter?"

"No, why should I? I don't know anyone in—" Then it hit her. "That was Celeste? That giggle?"

"I think you'll be surprised what love has done for our *Grand-mère*."

They walked up the narrow stairs with the threadbare carpet to the gallery that surrounded the auditorium. The walls had been draped with luxurious silks and velvets in deep, rich colors, and Celeste and Doc were busy hanging the photographs Celeste had brought with her from New Orleans.

Although the opera house was in poor repair, enough funds had been raised to patch the roof, damaged during the hurricane, so the photos and artifacts would remain dry.

Celeste turned at the sound of the creaky stairs, and her face lit up with the sweetest of smiles. "Melanie, *mon petit chou,* what a surprise. Did that husband of yours actually unchain you from the kitchen?"

The two women hugged. "*Grand-mère,* you know the kitchen is where I want to be most of the time."

Celeste pulled away from the hug. "Melanie, I want you to meet someone. This is Dr. Michel Landry, a very old and very dear friend."

"How do you do, Dr. Landry?" Melanie shook Doc's hand, polite as could be, while her eyes searched his face for some sign of duplicity.

"My pleasure," Doc said with a grin and a twinkle in

his eye. "Now, you can call me Doc, everyone else does."

Luc could see Melanie was immediately taken in by the older man's charm and obvious sincerity. Celeste dragged her around, showing her the various photographs, proud that she was donating the future museum's very first collection.

Doc, meanwhile, took Luc aside. "Any change in the status?"

"You mean with Loretta? No, she won't return my calls. She didn't even deliver any muffins this morning."

"You can't let her put you off forever. Take it from me, you don't want to be an octogenarian, wondering what could have been."

"I haven't given up, if that's what you're thinking." However long it took—another year, five years, ten— he would prove that he'd changed, that he was not like her first husband.

When he realized the direction his thoughts had just taken, he was so surprised his knees went weak. He lowered himself to a nearby folding chair so he could think it through without falling over.

He was in love with Loretta. There was no other explanation. If he was ready to spend the rest of his life in Indigo, proving he was worthy of her—that didn't sound like a crush or infatuation or some passing fancy.

"Luc? You all right? Your face just went white."

He shook his head. "I don't know if I'll ever be all right again. I'm afraid that woman has ruined me for good."

Celeste and Melanie returned from their "museum

tour," chattering like a couple of teenagers making plans for a big Friday night. "C'mon, Luc," Melanie said. "Up, up, up. I need to see Loretta's cooking facilities. Where is she, anyway? I thought this dinner was her bailiwick."

Celeste and Doc exchanged a worried look.

"I took it over," Luc said. "Loretta has too many things to do."

"But she's still going to let me use her kitchen, right?"

Celeste took Melanie's hand. "I'll walk over to the bakery with you, dear. I believe Luc and Michel have some business to take care of."

Luc shot his grandmother a grateful look. The last thing he wanted was to barge in on Loretta unannounced and have her go ballistic on him. Melanie didn't even know Luc and Loretta had been together, much less that they'd split up. It still surprised him that Celeste didn't use his disastrous romance as a platform to criticize him or compare him to his father. But she hadn't made a single negative comment.

Love really was transformative, as Loretta had pointed out on their one and only date. *He* was certainly a different man from the one he'd been when he'd arrived in Indigo. He'd come here counting the months until he'd be free. Now his freedom meant little. He'd just as soon be tied down to Indigo forever. But what were the chances?

FOR THE FIRST TIME in weeks, Loretta was caught up. She had the vendors lined up for the music festival. They'd all signed the appropriate contracts and returned them to her. They'd finished wrangling over the size of their signs and the locations of their booths, and the fact the festival had an exclusive contract with one soft drink megacorporation and couldn't serve drinks from the other.

She'd finished baking three pies of different varieties for tonight's bingo game at the church. They only needed to be boxed up. She'd swept and mopped and polished everything in sight, and she had nothing left to do—except think about Luc.

She alternated between being furious with him, and then all weepy, though she somehow managed to hold herself together whenever a customer came in. One woman had walked out without buying anything after accusing Loretta of having a cold and spreading her germs all over the baked goods.

She was in her own kitchen in the house, washing dishes from last night, when she heard the bell on the bakery door jangle. She quickly dried her hands and hurried out, then stopped short when she saw Celeste Robichaux and Melanie Marchand.

Panic rose in her throat. What did they want?

She schooled her face to reveal no emotion. "May I help you?"

"Oh, Loretta, your bakery is absolutely adorable!" Melanie enthused, coming forward to squeeze Loretta's cold hands. "I love how you built it onto the front of your house. How convenient, to just roll out of bed and right to work!"

"It is convenient," Loretta said, warming slightly. It

was hard to be cold around Melanie, since she was so friendly herself. And she was doing Loretta a heckuva favor. She would do well to remember that.

"I just came to check out your cooking facilities, for the dinner," Melanie said, her gaze focused on the wood-burning stove, which dominated one corner of the bakery.

"Please, make yourself at home. Anything you need, it's yours. And don't hesitate if you need me to purchase anything special—long as it doesn't break my budget."

"Luc's pretty much got everything covered." Melanie could resist no longer. The oven drew her toward it. "Where did you get this fabulous oven?"

"My father and I built it. Well, mostly my dad, but I helped. The door is an antique we scavenged from a junkyard."

"It's absolutely awe-inspiring. No wonder your breads are so fantastic. I want to buy some before I leave."

"Please, you can take whatever you want."

Celeste hadn't said a word. She'd seated herself at the scarred oak table and watched Loretta with curious, probing eyes.

Clearly Celeste knew what had happened between Loretta and Luc, but Melanie didn't have a clue.

"Would you ladies like some tea?" Loretta asked. Her quarrel wasn't with Luc's grandmother or his cousin, after all.

"I'd love some," Melanie said, just as Celeste issued a stern, "No, thank you."

Fine. Of course Celeste's loyalties would lie with her

grandson. But did she have to be so unpleasant about it? Who was the wronged party here? Who'd been deceived?

Or…the thought occurred to her as she moved through the familiar motions of brewing a pot of tea for Melanie, perhaps Celeste didn't know of Luc's…escapades. Maybe he had lied to his grandmother about his criminal past, and about their breakup. He could have told her anything.

Loretta tried to give the woman the benefit of the doubt. She set the teapot on the table, along with two mugs, sugar, lemon and cream. "There's a second mug there, Celeste, if you change your mind.

"Thank you, but no."

Loretta decided tiptoeing around the subject was too difficult. "Celeste, just because Luc and I are no longer together doesn't mean you and I can't be friends."

Celeste looked startled by Loretta's direct words, and for a moment she didn't know what to say.

Melanie just looked uncomfortable.

"Sorry, Melanie," Loretta said. "You shouldn't get stuck in the middle of this. Your cousin and I were briefly…an item. But that's no longer the case."

"Someone probably should have warned you," Melanie said. "Luc is a charmer. Women always fall all over him. It must be hard for a guy like that to be, you know, steady."

"Luc's steadiness is not the issue," Celeste said. "There are no other women, and there haven't been any other women. Not since he moved to Indigo."

"Then what's the problem?" Melanie asked.

Now Loretta desperately wished she hadn't brought

up the subject of Luc. "I'd rather not get into it," she said, but her objection had no effect.

"The problem," Celeste declared, "is Luc's criminal record. I advised Luc to be honest with her. He was going to tell her after the music festival, but unfortunately, she found out by other means."

"Oh." Melanie busied herself pouring tea.

Just then the front door burst open, and Zara whirled in like a dust devil, head down. "Hi, Mama. Bye, Mama." She tried to make her escape, not even acknowledging her new friend, "Tante Celeste."

"Zara, hold on."

Zara didn't stop. "I have to go to the bathroom."

Sensing something was up, Loretta practically chased her daughter down, catching her just before she reached the door leading out of the bakery and into the house. She caught her by the straps of her backpack and swiveled her around.

Zara had a black eye.

"Zara, what happened?"

"I'm not telling."

"You better tell me."

"It's your fault!" Zara cried. "You told me I could go fishing with Luc and I told everybody at school and then you changed your mind and I told Kiki and then she told everybody and Thomas said I was a big fat liar and I kicked him and he punched me in the face."

A host of emotions bombarded Loretta—anger that her daughter was still fighting, fury that a little boy would punch her baby in the face, guilt for being the root cause of the conflict.

Mother's guilt won out. "Oh, Zara."

Loretta tried to hug her daughter, but Zara would have none of it. "I don't want to be hugged right now. I'm mad and I want to be mad for a while."

This was new. "O-okay, honey."

Zara stalked out of the bakery, and Loretta let her go.

Celeste and Melanie were pretending not to listen, but there was no way they could have missed any detail of the argument. She returned to them.

"You see what I'm dealing with?"

Celeste stood up decisively. "Loretta, I'm sure you think you're being a good mother. But the least you could do is make a small effort to find out what happened with Luc."

"It doesn't matter. Unless he was falsely convicted. He wasn't, was he?"

Celeste wouldn't meet her gaze. "No. He committed a crime. But there were extenuating circumstances."

"I know all about extenuating circumstances. Jim, my husband, had a basket full of them. He was always blaming someone else for his bad behavior. But excuses didn't save him from going to prison, and they didn't save him from being murdered himself."

"Oh, jeez," Melanie murmured.

"I'm sorry," Loretta said. "This conversation has gotten completely out of hand. Can we forget about it and move on, please?" she pleaded.

"Of course," Celeste replied, ever polite. "But let me pass along a bit of wisdom—and at eighty-five years old, I'm allowed my wisdom. Forgiveness is a powerfully healing emotion. Just think about that for a few days. Melanie, come." She got up from the table and regally sailed out of the bakery.

Melanie gave a parting shrug and an apologetic smile as she followed her grandmother into the crisp autumn afternoon.

CHAPTER FIFTEEN

MELANIE STAYED long enough to have an early dinner before heading back to New Orleans, and Celeste and Doc joined them. Everyone tried to make it a festive occasion—for Luc's sake, he guessed, because by now they all knew Loretta had dumped him. He wasn't sure how Melanie had found out, but he could see that she had in every look she gave him.

Luc tried to get into the spirit of things as Doc made them up a batch of his famous mint juleps. He and Melanie put together a killer gumbo and some dirty rice. But he couldn't help thinking how much more fun it would have been if Loretta and Zara had joined them. Maybe Vincent and Adele, too.

A family get-together, the kind he'd never had in his life.

He tried to console himself with the knowledge that he did have a family. Celeste and Melanie had warmed up to him, and Doc might as well be a relative, as much as he hung around. And his mother would love him no matter what he did. All in all he was luckier than a lot of people.

He managed to keep up his end of the conversation,

talking about his future renovation plans for the second outbuilding. He'd been thinking about turning it into a workshop, where guests could try their hand at candle- and soap-making or canning—some type of participatory museum to reflect what times were like when the Creole cabin had been built.

"So do you think you'll keep working here?" Melanie asked innocently. "After the probation's up, I mean."

Luc shrugged. "I'll work here as long as *Grand-mère* wants me to. But I think she may have some plans of her own regarding the B and B."

Celeste nearly choked on her coffee. "What makes you say that?"

He gave her a knowing look. "Just a feeling."

LATER, WHEN MELANIE had gone home and the guests were all in their rooms, Luc couldn't help but ponder his future. Celeste had neither confirmed nor denied any plans for herself or the B and B, but Luc could see the writing on the wall. Celeste had been building her nest ever since she arrived.

Luc would only be in the way here.

But he would stay in Indigo. He felt at home here. If Loretta disapproved—if the whole town found out about his past and wanted to tar and feather him and ride him out of town—he would simply have to prove to them that he was a changed man.

LORETTA WAS AT her wit's end with her daughter. She'd tried love and tenderness and coddling, to no avail.

She'd tried tough love. She'd tried a sensible, talking-things-out approach. Zara was like a stone wall.

Zara's teacher had called. Apparently there were numerous witnesses to the fight at the school, and the consensus was that Thomas had deliberately provoked Zara, getting right in her face and taunting her until she'd lashed out. Then he'd thrown her to the ground and punched her—retribution for the previous fight.

But even when Loretta had told Zara she wasn't in trouble—well, not too much—Zara hadn't responded with anything but monosyllables, and she'd only picked at her dinner.

Something more than the fight was bothering her, but she claimed she was fine.

Loretta had thought she would have at least a few more years of peace before getting hit with attitude.

The next morning, when Zara still wasn't back to her usual cheerful self, Loretta was ready to tear out her hair. Given that she hadn't been sleeping well herself, she wasn't at her most patient. She set Zara's cereal in front of her and said, "Zara, I'm tired of this. If you don't tell me what's wrong, how can I fix it?"

"You can't fix it. You won't fix it."

"Fix what?"

"I want to be friends with Luc again."

There was no way around it. She was going to have to tell Zara the truth. Once her daughter realized Luc was not the saint she believed him to be, she would understand.

"I found out that Luc is a criminal."

Zara's eyes widened with disbelief. "You mean like a bank robber or something?"

"Or something."

"What did he do?"

"Well, I don't know exactly."

"Then how do you know it was bad?"

"Because he's on probation. That means he's serving a punishment for a serious crime."

"Maybe it wasn't his fault or something." Zara was grasping at straws. "Maybe someone made him do it. Maybe it was a mistake."

Loretta put her head in her hands. She was making everything worse.

"Couldn't you just ask him what he did?" Zara said. The suggestion sounded remarkably sensible.

"If I find out what crime he committed, and we agree it was bad, will you accept my decision that we should stay away from him?"

Zara didn't answer for a long time, and when she finally did, she said, "He didn't do anything that bad. I know he didn't. He's not like Jim."

"Honey, you don't even remember Jim. He could be sweet and thoughtful and charming, just like Luc. Just because a man is handsome and kind and charming on the outside doesn't mean you know what's on the inside."

"*I* know."

And it hadn't escaped Loretta's attention that Zara hadn't agreed to steer clear of Luc if they found out that the crime he'd committed was of a serious nature.

"Hurry up and eat. We need to get going." She was already running late with her deliveries, although now that she didn't linger at La Petite Maison over Luc's delicious coffee, her morning rounds didn't take as long.

She'd just have to learn how to make her own damn coffee.

LATER THAT MORNING, when she'd returned from her deliveries, Loretta made a phone call she was dreading. But it had to be done.

"Hotel Marchand, how may I direct your call?"

"Could I speak with Melanie Marchand, please? This is Loretta Castille."

A couple of minutes later, Melanie came on the line. "Hi, Loretta. What's up?" She sounded warm and friendly, though surely by now she'd been brought up to date on the idiotic soap opera that was Loretta's love life.

"I need to ask you something. Could you please tell me what Luc did to get a criminal conviction?"

Melanie paused a long time before answering. "Why don't you ask Luc?"

"Because I want the truth."

"He would tell you the truth, Loretta. I'm sure of that."

"Well, I'm not sure, and I have my reasons."

"It's not my place to tell you," Melanie said firmly. "But you should know this. I believe with all my heart that Luc regrets his actions."

"All criminals are sorry—when they get caught." She thought again of Jim, of the first time he'd been arrested for stealing a car. He'd stood up in court and claimed he'd learned his lessons. He had a baby on the way, he was worried about how he was going to take care of it. There hadn't been a dry eye in the courtroom.

He'd gotten a slap on the wrist, and two months later he'd stolen another car.

"Talk to Luc," Melanie said. "Find out what he has to say. Then you can judge him all you want."

"I'll think about it," Loretta replied, although she knew she wouldn't. "Thanks for taking the time to talk to me."

She knew she was being harsh. But she also knew what a pushover she was, how vulnerable she was to Luc's charms. What if he convinced her that whatever he'd done was a terrible mistake, that he was now completely reformed? She would get back together with him, and then he would do something awful and she would never, ever be able to forgive herself.

She'd taken Jim back twice, believing he was sincere, until he'd held up a convenience store and shot the clerk.

If not for Zara, she wasn't sure how she would have survived that period of her life. She wouldn't put herself through it again.

AT THREE-TWENTY, Loretta got a call from Della Roy, the school bus driver. "Loretta, I just wanted to let you know that Zara didn't get on the bus today."

"What? Oh, shoot, not again." This wasn't the first time Zara had missed the bus. It wasn't her day for Girl Explorers, but maybe she'd gotten involved in a game after school. "Thanks, Della, I'll have to go track her down, I guess." She hated to close the bakery when she had a steady stream of customers coming in, but she couldn't let her child run wild over the countryside with no supervision.

It didn't occur to her to be worried.

But when she arrived at the school, no one there had seen Zara or had any idea where she might be. Mrs. Brainard, who was still in her classroom straightening up, said there'd been no trouble from Zara that day, though she'd been more quiet than usual.

"Maybe she went home with a friend," Loretta said as a small bubble of anxiety floated up from her sub-conscious. "Sometimes she forgets to ask permission." Or maybe she got permission and Loretta had completely forgotten about it, like the day Zara had ridden her bike to the B and B, ostensibly to catch crawfish. She racked her brain, but couldn't remember arranging any play dates for today.

Then a thought occurred to her. Could she have gone to the B and B to see Luc? Knowing Zara, she would ask him point-blank to give her an accounting of his criminal record. But La Petite Maison was too far to walk easily from school. She might have gotten a ride from someone, though.

The more she thought about it, the more likely that scenario was, although if the mother of one of Zara's friends had given her a lift, surely the woman would have made Zara phone home to tell Loretta. She would have to drive over to Luc's and check.

She got in her car and drove to the other side of town, her stomach in knots. She wouldn't panic about Zara. Her daughter had missed the bus before and there was always a reasonable explanation, at least to Zara's way of thinking.

When she pulled into the drive, she saw that Luc's Tahoe was in the carport. She walked to the front door and rang the bell. Slipping in the kitchen door seemed too casual under the circumstances.

Celeste answered, her face neutral. "Loretta. What brings you here?"

"I'm sorry to bother you, but Zara is missing, and I wondered if she'd by chance come here after school."

"Missing?" Celeste's face immediately softened into an expression of concern. "*Mon Dieu,* no, I haven't seen her. Luc is down by the dock working on the boat, if you'd like to ask him."

"Yes, I'll do that." Maybe Zara had seen Luc and wandered down to talk to him. Loretta walked briskly along the brick path toward the bayou. She would quickly check for Zara and then leave immediately.

She saw the boat before she saw Luc. The faded canopy was gone, replaced with a bright new one sporting blue and white stripes. Now that it was clean and freshly painted, the boat was quite beautiful. She found it hard to believe this was the same filthy vessel he'd started with.

Then she saw Luc, and her breath caught in her throat. He was behind the boat, wearing a pair of waders and up to his knees in swamp muck as he worked to scrape the *Bitchin' Mama* decal off the stern. Although it wasn't particularly warm today, he'd taken off his shirt. His muscles flexed as he wielded the scraper, and his hair gleamed gold in the afternoon sun.

"Luc?"

He turned, startled. "Loretta." He didn't smile a greeting, but why would he? After she'd repeatedly hung up on him and erased his messages without listening to them, he didn't even owe her common courtesy.

"I'm sorry to bother you, but have you seen Zara?"

"No. But you might ask Celeste—"

"I already did."

"Is she missing?"

"She wasn't on the bus, but it's no big deal. She probably went off with a friend and forgot to tell me." She tried not to sound terribly concerned, but the anxiety in her voice betrayed her.

He laid down his tools and came out of the water to stand on the muddy bank. "It must be a big deal, or you wouldn't have come this close to me."

He had her there. "Zara and I argued last night—about you. She's just a little girl, she doesn't understand. I thought she might have come here looking for better answers than the ones I've been giving her."

"I haven't seen her. But I'll help you look for her."

"That's not necessary," Loretta said quickly, but he was already peeling off the waders. "I'm sure she'll turn up soon."

"In which case I'll be very relieved and feel silly for worrying. But I'm going to look for her, anyway."

He obviously wasn't concerned whether she wanted him to search or not. She had to admire the way he'd dropped everything to help. It had nothing to do with trying to get back in her good graces, either. He was worried.

He shoved his arms into the sleeves of his denim workshirt as he walked. "Have you called her friends?"

"Not yet. I'll go back home and see if she's there. If not, I'll get out the school directory and start calling."

"I'll drive around town, then. If she's playing outside somewhere, I'll spot her. What was she wearing?"

Loretta had to think for a moment. "Blue jeans. Red-and-blue striped sweater. White sneakers. Try the park, and the general store. Oh, and the diner. Call me on my cell if you find her."

"You'll do likewise?"

"Yes. I'll let you know."

Luc stepped inside the house to tell Celeste what he was doing. By the time Loretta got her station wagon started, he was already striding toward his car, keys in hand, a very determined look on his face.

God help her, but she was happy to have him on her side. Only a man of character would drop everything to look for an AWOL nine-year-old. But men of character didn't go out and get themselves arrested for felonies. It just didn't make sense.

LUC PICTURED the map of Indigo in his head and worked his way methodically along the streets, looking for a flash of red. He stopped at the park and asked a group of older kids playing soccer if they'd seen her, but no one had. He checked the general store to see if she'd stopped in to buy candy or soda, but again, no one had seen her. Nor had she dropped into the Blue Moon Diner for a piece of pie.

He kept looking, hoping his phone would ring and Loretta would let him know that Zara was home safe and sound, that he'd panicked for nothing. But the phone remained frighteningly silent.

The town of Indigo was pretty small, so Luc covered all the streets in a very short time. He ventured farther out, onto the back roads. All the while, terrible images played in his head—accidents, kidnappings, drownings.

As it was getting dark, he headed back to town. His intention was to stop by the bakery and find out what else he could do to help.

But as he neared the center of town, he saw the flashing blue-and-red lights of a squad car—Alain's car—and his heart almost stopped beating altogether. This wasn't good.

He pulled in behind the squad car and got out. Alain and a couple of other men were searching around the opera house with flashlights.

"Alain," Luc called.

Indigo's police chief turned to him. "Luc. You haven't seen Zara Castille, have you?"

Luc's heart sank. "No. Why are you focusing here?"

"Take a look." He shone his flashlight against the side wall of the opera house. Someone had grafittied the native stone with red paint, and the perpetrator hadn't gone out of her way to conceal her identity, either. The wall now boldly advertised, ZARA CASTILLE WAS HERE.

"Oh, Zara," he murmured. Talk about taking a bid for

attention to the extreme. To Alain he said, "I've got a flashlight in my car. I'll help you look."

Since the other men were focusing their search around the opera house, Luc walked across the expansive green lawn, which was dotted with shrubs and stone benches, behind the building. The others had shied away from searching near the bayou—perhaps unconsciously fearing what they might find. But Luc knew Zara wouldn't get close enough to risk drowning.

She was around here somewhere, hiding, watching the chaos she'd caused. He'd bet his life on it.

"Zara!" He shined his flashlight into the cypress trees that looked spookier than usual as darkness fell. His beam of light played in and out of the Spanish moss.

"Luc!"

Luc nearly jumped out of his skin. His name, a whisper on the wind, had come from the shrub he'd just passed.

He whirled around. "Zara?"

"I'm here."

And so she was, concealed almost perfectly. She no longer wore red-and-blue stripes, but a camouflage sweatshirt. Her bright hair was bundled under a brown knit hat.

Luc's first feeling was one of intense relief, followed quickly by a surge of anger. He wanted to reach down and yank the little delinquent out from that bush, throw her over his shoulder and turn her over to Alain. But she looked scared, so he curbed his temper. "What are you doing hiding there?"

"Don't be mad, Luc. I did it for you."

That was just what he needed to hear. In addition to despising him, Loretta would probably have him arrested for contributing to the delinquency of a minor. "Come out from that bush."

"I have a plan. Don't spoil it."

"You have exactly five seconds to get out from those bushes or I'm coming in after you. One, two, three—"

"Oh, all right. But don't you even want to hear my plan?" The dense shrub trembled and rustled and finally parted until Zara emerged. She'd painted brown splotches on her face and the backs of her hand. Pretty damn clever way to hide.

He grabbed her hand and started for the opera house, walking a little too fast, practically dragging the child. "Do you have any idea how worried everyone is? Your mother must be frantic by now."

"Have you talked to her?"

"I did earlier, and she was plenty worried then." Luc waved his flashlight to get Alain's attention. "I found her!"

Alain rushed up to her, then practically fell to his knees to visually inspect her. "Zara, arc you all right?" He brushed at her cheek with his finger. "What have you got all over you?"

"Camel-flage."

"Where've you been? Everyone was so worried." He enveloped the girl in a bear hug. Alain and Zara were close, since he'd been teaching her how to play the fiddle. But Zara still looked a little dumbfounded by the display of emotion.

"I've just been…around. But Mr. Luc found me. Doesn't that make him a hero or something?"

"Can't thank you enough, Luc," Alain said. "How did you know where to look?"

"Er, I didn't. She kind of found me." Zara's plan, at least part of it, was gradually becoming apparent to Luc. She was hoping her mother would be so grateful to Luc for finding her missing daughter that she would stop being mad at him.

Nice thought, but it probably wasn't going to work.

"Zara," Alain said after he'd rounded up the other searchers and let them know the child was safe, "did you paint the wall of the opera house?"

"Uh-huh."

He sighed. "I'm gonna call your mama and let her know you're safe. Then we'll figure out what to do next." He led her to his squad car and put her in the front seat with a stern order for her to stay put.

Luc followed, and while Alain was on the phone, he took the opportunity to question Zara. He opened the car door and leaned down, propping his elbow on the roof. "Why did you do that?" He pointed to the defaced stone wall. "That building is a historical landmark."

"I did it because I'm a juvenile delinquent." She struggled a bit over the words, but she got them out.

"Zara, do you know what happens to juvenile delinquents?"

"They don't go to jail, do they?" She was starting to look frightened.

"Sometimes they get arrested," Luc said, "and sometimes they go to jail. But the worst thing is that they make their mothers really, really sad. How do you think your mother is going to feel about this?"

Zara did seem troubled by this notion, but she also looked determined. "She'll want to do what's best for me."

Alain opened the driver's door and slid behind the wheel. "Come on, Zara, I'll take you home."

"Can't Luc take me home?"

"I have to talk to your mother and explain what you did. Then we have to figure out what's to be done."

Luc gave Zara's shoulder a reassuring squeeze, then closed the door, his heart heavy. He was afraid Loretta and Zara were in for some tough times. It wouldn't even surprise him if Loretta thought he had put Zara up to this stunt, just to turn himself into a hero.

His last view of Zara was her painted face looking forlornly at him through the car window, her little hand pressed against the glass. She would learn, and soon enough, that he was not a hero in anyone's eyes. Especially not his own.

CHAPTER SIXTEEN

LORETTA HUNG UP the phone, relief coursing through her veins like a drug. "She's okay. That was Alain. He's bringing her home."

Adele's eyes filled with tears of relief, and Vincent crossed himself in thanks. "So what happened? Where's she been?"

"Making mischief, apparently. We'll get it all sorted out when she gets here."

They didn't have to wait long. Soon the lights of Alain's patrol car shone through the bakery's front windows. Loretta couldn't wait—she ran out the door and to the car, and when the passenger door opened and her little girl scrambled out, Loretta scooped her up and held her tightly.

"Oh, baby, I was so scared. Are you sure you're okay?"

"I'm okay. Luc found me."

Loretta looked to Alain for confirmation.

"It was Luc who found her," Alain said. They went back inside, where Loretta got her subdued daughter something to eat as Alain explained the evening's events.

"Luc saw the commotion and stopped to help. He

found Zara hiding in some bushes down near the bayou."

Luc. She was going to have to do something about him. But first things first. "Zara," she said, trying not to sound too accusatory, "can you tell us why you went to all this trouble?"

"Because I'm a juvenile delinquent. I come from a broken home."

Loretta definitely smelled something fishy here. Zara had an agenda. And Loretta had a pretty good idea what it was.

Alain sat down next to Zara at the oak table. "You know, Zara, what I've found is, it's not so much the number of parents that makes for a good home to raise a child in, but the amount of love and care and concern and guidance the child gets. And everyone in town knows that your mama, and your grandparents, too, give you enough love for ten kids. So I'm not buying this 'broken home' nonsense."

"Thank you, Alain," Loretta said, "but I think I know what's going on. Zara's on a campaign to convince me she needs a father."

"Ahhh. Well, Zara, honcy, I'm sure your mama would like you to have a father, too. But you can't just buy one at the store."

"I know that," Zara said. "But I know where she can get one."

Alain quickly pushed his chair back. "I think this investigation is no longer in my area of expertise."

"Do I have to go to jail?" Zara asked, sounding scared but a little intrigued by the possibility.

"No, but you'll need to clean up that wall you painted."

"It's just tempera paint," Zara said. "It'll come off with water."

Well, that was a relief, at least. "We'll take care of it tomorrow," Loretta told Alain. "And I'll come up with an additional punishment, just so Zara's clear on the consequences of breaking the law."

"Mama—"

"Not a word out of you, missy." Now that the surge of relief was wearing off, Loretta's anger rose.

Alain nodded. "I'm sure you'll do what's best. And I'm just awful glad no harm came to you, Miss Zara." He tipped his hat and went on his way.

Zara hadn't eaten much of her dinner, but Loretta wasn't in the mood to argue about it. "Are you finished here?"

She nodded.

"Then go take a bath and get all that paint off you. Afterward, it's straight to bed."

"Yes, ma'am." She slipped out of her chair and headed forlornly toward the house.

"Wait. Zara…"

Zara stopped, and Loretta went to her and enveloped her in yet another bear hug. "No matter what happens, no matter what you do, I'll always love you. I'm put out with you right now, but I still love you. Okay?"

She nodded. "I love you, too."

"Mama," Loretta said, "do you think you could supervise her bath for me? And shampoo her hair? She's got paint in it."

"Of course."

"I have something important to do."

Adele nodded, understanding perfectly. Vincent just looked pleased. "We'll spend the night here, if you need us to," he said. "Don't worry about a thing. But you might, um…do something about your own hair."

Well, that told her where her parents stood on the issue of Luc. They hadn't pushed her one way or another when they'd learned of the breakup, but they'd obviously been hoping she would change her mind about Luc.

She checked herself in the car's rearview mirror and realized her father had a point. She looked a fright, as if she'd been struck by lightning or something. She ran her fingers through her hair, then dug in her purse for some lipstick, but she gave up after a fruitless search. Luc would just have to take her as she was.

If he didn't slam the door in her face on principle alone.

When she pulled up to the B and B, lights shone warmly through the windows. It was such a beautiful, inviting home, and Luc was the soul of it. A person who had created such a place from the ground up had to be good, deep-down good.

She was distressed that Luc's car wasn't there. She walked to the front door and rang the bell, and Celeste answered. The woman didn't look quite as formidable as usual. Maybe she'd softened, too.

"Celeste, is Luc here?" Loretta asked.

"No, I'm sorry, dear. He left a while ago, didn't say where he was going. But he seemed in a…melancholy mood. Would you like to come in and wait for him?"

"Yes, thank you." Celeste opened the door wider and

allowed Loretta to step into the warmth. As always, the B and B smelled wonderful—like home.

"Michel made us some mulled wine," Celeste said. "We're enjoying it with some of the guests in the parlor. You can join us if you like."

"I'm afraid I wouldn't be very good company. I'll just sit in the kitchen."

"All right, dear."

Celeste walked her to the kitchen, which was permeated with the heady scent of mulled wine simmering in a Crock-Pot. She refilled her cup, then got one for Loretta. Loretta blew on it, then took an appreciative sip. "This is delicious, thank you."

Amiable conversation and laughter drifted in from the lounge, but surprisingly, Celeste didn't rejoin the group. She pulled out the chair opposite Loretta and sat down.

"I apologize for my behavior yesterday," Celeste said. "It was a knee-jerk reaction toward someone I perceived had hurt one of my cubs."

Loretta smiled at the thought of Luc as a cub.

"I found out less than two years ago that I had a grandson," Celeste continued. "And I'll confess, the initial impression he made on me wasn't favorable. But I've kept an eye on him. And I've come to realize what a good heart he has. At one time in his life, he was misguided—but that was partly my fault, too."

"Luc has to be responsible for his own actions," Loretta said.

"And believe me, he has taken responsibility. Not like his father, not at all."

"Luc's father got into trouble, too?"

"To put it mildly. Pierre, my son, was a rough-and-tumble little boy, always in trouble, and I simply refused to tolerate him. I expected him to be just like his older sister—demure, obedient, perfectly behaved. The harder I clamped down on him, the worse his behavior became. But I never made any attempt to understand him.

"By the time he was a teenager, it was open warfare. And he left home as soon as he was able—and I never saw him again."

"That must have been terrible," Loretta said, feeling a bond with Celeste as a mother. "I don't know what I would do if Zara left me."

"I pretended it didn't bother me, but of course it did. For a short while he communicated with Anne, his sister, unbeknownst to me, and she tried to talk him back home. But his story was that I'd kicked him out and disowned him. And, looking back, I can see how he might have seen things that way. I was incredibly harsh, but I guess that's what I thought the boy needed. I never dreamed he would disappear for good."

"We all do the best we can," Loretta said. "Being a parent is the hardest job on earth."

"I'm telling you this not to get your sympathy, but to provide some background that you might find useful when you talk to Luc."

"Thank you."

Car lights coming up the driveway signaled Luc's return, and Celeste quickly stood. But she didn't leave right away. She poured yet another cup of the mulled wine and set it on the table. "Give Luc this. It loosens the tongue and mellows the mood, as I've just proved."

By the time Luc walked through the kitchen door, Celeste had gone. "Loretta." He had on an old, beat-up leather jacket and his most faded jeans, making him look the perfect rebel. The cautious, guarded expression on his face fit perfectly with the image.

"Luc." Earlier, she'd been burning with things she wanted to tell him, but now that the moment had arrived, she was strangely bereft of words. Well, there was one easy thing she could start with. "Thank you for finding Zara."

Luc shrugged. "Like I told Alain, she pretty much found me. She wanted me to be a hero."

"You *are* a hero. Not everyone would drop whatever they were doing to look for a missing child—especially the missing child of a woman who's been so horrible to you."

"Whatever piece of bad road you and I have traveled, I wasn't going to hold it against Zara."

"No, you wouldn't." She extended the cup of wine toward him. "Celeste says you should drink some of this. It'll loosen your tongue and mellow your mood."

"Is there more to say?"

She nodded and swallowed, her mouth suddenly dry. This was even harder than she'd thought it would be. "I'm sorry for the way I've acted."

"It's your business if you don't want anything to do with a convicted felon. Especially given your history."

"Maybe. But that's not a decision I should make without knowing the whole story. You wanted to tell me, and I wouldn't let you, and that was wrong."

He accepted the wine and took a big gulp, then looked at it, surprised. "What is this stuff?"

"Mulled wine. Michel made it."

"That explains the kick." He pulled out a chair and sat down. "Loretta, if you want the whole story, I'll tell you. Every sordid detail. I wanted to tell you before, but you were so stressed out about the music festival, I figured you had enough on your plate. But I planned to tell you right after the festival. Even though I knew it might end our relationship."

"So tell me now."

"I don't know that it will make any difference. I did some terrible things."

She knew she had to hear what those things were. A part of her wanted to tell him it didn't matter, she would love him no matter what. But she'd been so stupidly trusting with Jim.

"I confess, I did panic when I discovered you had a record," she said, "because all I could think about was Jim—sticking up a convenience store and shooting a man because he didn't open the cash register fast enough. But you're not Jim. And I can't imagine you did *anything* like rob someone."

He didn't immediately reassure her he hadn't, which gave her only a slight unease. This was Luc, sweet, kind Luc.

"I'll tell you the whole story," he said. "Do you mind if we get comfortable first? It's kind of long."

They moved to Luc's quarters, where, for lack of any other place to settle, they sat on the bed. Luc stretched out, propped up with some pillows, and Loretta slipped off her shoes and sat cross-legged, still clutching her mug of mulled wine.

"I already told you about my father," Luc began. "How he made peace with my mom and me before he died. But that wasn't the whole story." He paused, as if he were looking back in time. "On his deathbed, he made me promise that I would claim the family legacy he'd been denied. His mother and sister and her family were worth millions, he figured, and he thought I should get my share. Or maybe, what he really said, was that I should make peace with them. My memories might be less than accurate, because I was pretty angry with his family. They'd given my father a raw deal."

"Celeste told me that part. It sounds like maybe he *was* treated unfairly."

"He brought it on himself," Luc insisted. "Pierre Robichaux was always the victim, always being wronged. But I didn't understand that at the time. I was a walking cliché—the angry young man.

"Still, I didn't do anything about it for a long time." Luc explained that he'd left home after his father's death and kicked around the world, talking his way into jobs at luxury hotels, leaving when he got bored.

Then he went to work for the Corbin brothers, who used their small hotels in Thailand to defraud people. When their crimes started to catch up to them, they decided to move back to the States and expand their business there.

Luc had found the perfect way to seek his revenge through the brothers' scheme to acquire a property in New Orleans' French Quarter. The Hotel Marchand, owned by his aunt, was ideal for their purposes, since it was already in financial trouble. Luc joined the staff as a concierge, and his job was to work from the inside to ruin the hotel's reputation so the owners would be forced to sell—at a bargain-basement price.

"And that's what you did?" Loretta found it nearly impossible to picture the Luc she knew doing something so hateful.

"I did," he confirmed. "At first, it was fairly innocuous. I tampered with the generator and it failed during a power outage. I mixed up reservations for a society wedding party, and I leaked a story to the tabloids about a celebrity staying with us."

"Oh, Luc."

"But almost from the beginning, I had a problem. I liked the Marchands. They treated me like family, even though they had no idea who I was. So I tried to back out of my agreement with the Corbin brothers. But it wasn't that easy. By then they were involved with some mobster types who didn't care who got hurt—or killed—so long as they got their hotel."

"And you didn't go to the police?"

"I finally did. Unfortunately, I went to the wrong cop. He was on the crime boss's payroll. I was shot by one of the Corbin brothers and left for dead."

Loretta gasped. This was far more sordid and complex than she'd imagined. No wonder Charlotte and Melanie Marchand had been so guarded around Luc when he'd gone to the hotel to talk about the Cajun dinner. "Oh, Luc. Is that how you got the scar on your back?"

He nodded. "I'm tough, though. The bullet nicked my liver and I lost a lot of blood, but I recovered. The important thing was that I was able to tell the police everything. By that time Charlotte and Jackson, who's now her husband, had been kidnapped. But the police were able to rescue them and arrests were made."

"Including you."

"Including me. But I turned state's evidence, and the Marchands actually came out in favor of leniency. I was charged with everything from fraud to conspiracy to theft to malicious mischief, but only the theft charge stuck. I got a two-year probated sentence, and if I stay out of trouble for five years, I can have my record expunged."

"Oh, Luc," she said again, sighing. "Is that everything?"

"That's everything. Except that it was Celeste's brilliant idea to send me here to make restitution to the family. She thought she was being pretty clever, condemning me to some backwater town. At first, I think she was hoping I wouldn't be able to hack it, and I'd mess up my probation and end up in jail, proving her theory that I was a bad seed, just like my father. Neither of us had any idea how much I would love it here."

Loretta was silent for a while, taking it all in. Luc was right, he'd done some pretty bad things. But she could feel his regret. And she could hear the fondness in his voice for his cousins, his aunt—even his grandmother.

"So," Luke said briskly. "You can run screaming into the night, now, if you want. I won't hold it against you."

She studied his face and saw the vulnerability there. Her heart squeezed painfully. "I have no intention of running. I feel exactly the same about you as I did before you told me. I don't care what you did. I can see with my own eyes that you're kind and generous and hard-working."

"Maybe you're seeing what you want to see," he said cautiously.

"No. You've made mistakes, but who hasn't? It doesn't mean I can't love you. Everyone deserves a second chance, a fresh start." She looked down at her empty cup. "Celeste was right about this stuff."

When she looked up, she felt dizzy from the intensity of Luc's gaze.

"Somewhere in all that," he said, "did you just say you loved me?"

"I did."

"You know I love you too, don't you?"

"N-not until right this moment." Love. But what did that word mean to Luc?

"I think I was in love with you months ago," he said, "but since I've never been in love before, I didn't recognize it."

"Love can be very sneaky." She reached her hand toward him, only to find he'd done the same to her. They clasped hands, and then somehow they were in each other's arms, lying in the middle of the bed, kissing as if they'd been lovers separated for years instead of a couple of days.

Pausing for breath, Luc pulled back and looked deeply into Loretta's eyes, stroking her hair. "I love you," he said again. "And I love Zara, too."

"I want you to spend as much time with Zara as you please. I know you'll be a good influence on her—for however long you choose to stay in Indigo." She forced herself to say that last part. But she knew she had to accept Luc exactly as he was, not the ideal she wanted him to be.

"However long? How about the next hundred years or so?"

"Luc, don't tease."

"I'm dead serious. I've never stayed in one place long because I've never had a reason to before. But I love this town. I love the people, the way they care so much about each other. I probably won't be in this house. I think *Grand-mère* intends to live here and run the place herself. But I'll find something to do. Maybe I'll run a swamp tour business."

Loretta could hardly believe what she was hearing. Luc here in Indigo, forever? She couldn't bear to think of La Petite Maison without Luc, but Celeste was the owner, and Loretta could understand the other woman's desire to run it. And whatever business Luc decided to get into, he would make it something wonderful.

Luc jostled her. "You still with me?"

She realized she'd been staring off into space. "No. I'm just speechless." She sat up and pulled away slightly, trying to gauge his sincerity. "You'll really stay here?"

He nodded. "And something else. I want to marry you. Now, you don't have to answer right away—"

"Yes."

"—because I'll keep asking. Maybe once a month or so."

"I said yes."

"You did?"

She leaned in and kissed him again. "Yes."

EPILOGUE

LUC HAD NEVER FELT so nervous in his life. Confessing his past sins to Loretta had been easy—like taking off a heavy jacket. But asking Zara how she felt about having a new dad, that was scary.

Loretta had assured him Zara would be wild about the idea. After all, that had been her master plan: to prove to her mother that she needed a father, Luc in particular, to divert her from a life of crime. But when faced with the reality of having a new authority figure, she might balk.

He dressed with care in his best blue chambray shirt and dress slacks. He was going to Loretta's to have his talk with Zara, then they were all coming back to the B and B for dinner. Vincent and Adele were invited, and of course Celeste and Doc would be there. Luc was going to announce his and Loretta's engagement.

If everything went according to plan.

He arrived at Loretta's at six-thirty. She let him in, looking sexier than ever in slinky black pants and a sheer, ruffled blouse with an enticingly low-cut neckline.

She greeted him with a warm kiss. "I have to warn

you—" But that was all she got to say. Zara came running full tilt into the bakery, screaming "Luc! Luc, Luc, Luc, you're here!" And she barreled into him, throwing her arms around his waist and squeezing so tight he worried she might never let go. "Luc, is it true, are you really going to be my daddy?"

Loretta shrugged. "I'm sorry, but she guessed right away and I'm not good at keeping secrets."

"I can keep secrets, I'm real good at it," Zara said. "Mama says I can't tell anyone till you make the 'noucement at dinner tonight." Finally she released Luc and beamed up at him with the sweetest smile.

"So you're okay with your mom and me getting married?"

"I can't wait! Can you do it tomorrow?"

"Not tomorrow, but soon," Luc promised. "Now, then, I still have something to say to you, young lady."

"Uh-oh."

"Yeah, uh-oh. What you did by running away and painting the wall of the opera house was a really bad thing to do. No matter how much you want things to go your way, you can't be thoughtless and hurtful to people you love. Do you know what I mean when I say the ends don't justify the means?"

"It means that even though my plan worked, it was still a bad plan and I shouldn't have done it."

"Exactly."

Zara chewed on a thumbnail. "I didn't know everyone would be so worried. I thought they would just be mad at me."

"Well, you need to think these things through."

"I have, and I'm really, really sorry. I cleaned up the paint, and I wrote a letter to Alain and every person who looked for me to say I was sorry. But Mama said that wasn't enough. She said I can't play my fiddle at the music festival."

"Your mama's a tough cookie. Believe me, I know."

"Don't you think it's unfair?" She blinked her big hazel eyes at Luc, and he had to force himself to firm his resolve.

"I think maybe next time you hatch a plan like the last one, you'll remember the consequences and think twice."

Zara's eyes shone with tears, but if she was hoping to play Luc against Loretta, it wasn't going to work. She sighed. "Okay."

"Zara," Loretta said, "run and put your good black shoes on. We have to leave in a few minutes."

Zara stamped out dejectedly.

"Did I do okay?" Luc asked.

Loretta smiled. "You did fine. But do you think I'm being too harsh, grounding her from the music festival? She's been rehearsing for weeks, and she's so good."

"Like I said, you're one tough cookie."

"Maybe I should think of another punishment."

They turned as one when they heard a noise coming from the house—soft, at first, then louder. It was Zara's fiddle, and she was playing the most melancholy song Luc had ever heard.

"Oh, now that's enough to break my heart," he said.

"Zara Castille, were you eavesdropping?" Loretta demanded.

The music stopped and Zara peeked around the corner. "Just a little bit, by accident." She ran back into the bakery, still barefoot, clutching her fiddle. "Oh, Mama, when you told me about Luc, you said everyone deserves a second chance. Don't you think I do, too? I'll do anything. I'll scrub the bakery floor every day, you can cut off my allowance for a year, burn all my Harry Potter cards, but please let me play my song in the festival."

Luc tried to keep a straight face. Only a stone could fail to respond to the child's plea, and Loretta was no stone.

"Oh, all right," she finally said. Zara hugged her and thanked her about ten times. "Now go put your shoes on!"

"Yes, ma'am!"

When they were alone again, Loretta looked at Luc, who was still trying to hide his amusement. "She's your problem now, too, you know."

He took her hand. "Everyone should be so lucky to have such a problem."

DINNER WAS FESTIVE and full of laughter. Luc had baked some chicken breasts and rosemary potatoes, and Doc had contributed a spicy Cajun corn salad. Loretta brought some crescent rolls and Vincent and Adele an apple pie. Celeste selected a couple of bottles of very good wine from the stash she'd brought with her.

As Adele cut the pie, Luc knew it was time to make his announcement. He hoped everyone would be happy—but he wasn't completely convinced. Now that Vincent and Adele knew he had a criminal record, they might not be too keen to have him as a son-in-law.

He drew in a breath, prepared to ask for everyone's attention, when Celeste beat him to it.

"Since we're all gathered here," she said, "I have an announcement to make."

Well, talk about stealing his thunder. Luc swallowed, almost grateful for the small reprieve.

"Luc, you have done an incredible job, not only with renovating this old cottage and bringing it back to its former glory, but in establishing the B and B and running it profitably. I confess, I expected you to fail. I was actually looking forward to it. I'm somewhat ashamed of my behavior toward you now that I see it in retrospect. You have proved yourself, more than proved yourself, and I am truly proud to call you my grandson."

"Thank you, *Grand-mère*." Here it comes, he thought. She was thanking him for services rendered, and now she was going to announce that she was taking over the B and B and he was out of a job.

"So I've made a decision. Several decisions, actually. I'm going to give you La Petite Maison. As a wedding present."

Luc's jaw dropped. He glanced over at Loretta, but she shrugged helplessly. "How did you know we're getting married?"

"You're not getting married," Celeste said imperiously. "*I'm* getting married. Or rather, Michel and I are. That's why Michel planned this dinner. Isn't it?"

"I thought *I* planned the dinner," Luc said. "To announce Loretta's and my engagement."

Vincent let loose with a hearty laugh. "Sounds like everyone's getting married!"

Then the rest of what his grandmother had said sank in. "*Grand-mère,* you really mean it? You want to give me the B and B? Won't the rest of the family object?"

"Anne and the girls are completely in favor of it. You're a part of our family. Your father didn't get a fair shake, and nothing can ever change that, but we all agreed you should have the B and B."

"I don't know what to say."

"Thank you would be appropriate."

Luc stepped around the table and wrapped his arms around his grandmother. She was stiff at first, but gradually she relaxed. "Thank you. You know, I was positive you came to Indigo to fire me and take over running the B and B yourself."

"Good heavens, what an awful idea. I've never worked for a living a day in my life. Why would I start at age eighty-five?"

"This calls for a toast," Doc said, refilling everyone's wineglasses. "Best wishes to the brides…" He lifted his glass to Loretta, then Celeste.

"And the grooms," Celeste finished for him, nodding toward Luc and Doc in turn. "Now doesn't this just prove that anyone, even a cranky old woman, can turn over a new leaf and make a fresh start?"

More toasts followed, along with plenty of hugs and tears. For the first time since he'd left the Hotel Marchand in disgrace, Luc felt a part of something larger than himself—a family, a community. He had real ties now, ties that could never be broken.

"I almost forgot," Doc said. "Who's up for a boat ride?"

"A boat ride?" Celeste echoed. "With all the wine we've had, who among us would dare pilot the boat?"

"Oh, all right, we don't have to actually ride in the boat. But we do have to go look at it."

"Michel, have you lost your mind?"

But Doc wouldn't be dissuaded, and they all abandoned their pie to troop outside and down the brick walkway. Luc grinned. With everything else that had happened the past couple of days, he'd forgotten this last surprise.

Loretta took his hand. "What's going on?" she asked. "You look like you know something."

"You'll see."

Luc's boat, looking spiffy even in the dark, bobbed gently on the water next to the dock. Doc shone his flashlight on the stern, where his surprise became apparent. The *Bitchin' Mama* was no more. Now the boat bore the name, *Celeste.*

"Oh, Michel." Celeste giggled like a schoolgirl.

"It was all Luc," Doc said.

"It's my present to you, *Grand-mère,*" Luc said. "For giving me the chance to start over. I know it's not much, but if you hadn't sent me here, I never would have met Loretta or Zara, and I might never have known what it was to belong somewhere, to be a part of something bigger than myself, and to love someone more than life itself."

Celeste dabbed at her eyes. "It's one of the nicest presents I've ever received. I've always wanted to be immortal."

* * * * *

"Well," Cally said, turning the glass, watching the ice dance, "maybe you should try another tactic. Like get to know him better."

"Get to know him better?" Marjo said as she spun around. "Yeah, I'll try that—with a twelve-gauge in my hands."

"Hey!" Cally put her hands up. "I'm a lawyer, remember? Don't be plotting a felony in front of me."

Marjo laughed. "I wouldn't *really* do that. It's just that everything he does seems destined to infuriate me. The man is like a nest of yellow jackets kicked up by some overeager teenager with a Weed Whacker."

Cally waved a finger at her. "Now, be nice, Marjo. You know the old saying—and you also know it wouldn't be an old saying if it weren't true. So if I were you, I'd try catching this fly with some honey. Add a little Savoy sweetener, get him to come around to your ideas about the opera house. That way, he'll not only leave, he won't try it again."

Marjo ran a finger over the rim of her glass, considering the idea. "You mean, get him to see why the opera house is so important."

"Yeah."

"I don't know. He doesn't strike me as the sentimental type."

Cally gave her a grin. "Then use your feminine wiles. If there's one thing that can turn a man from alligator to teddy bear, it's a pretty woman with a smile."

REQUEST YOUR FREE BOOKS!

2 FREE NOVELS
FROM THE SUSPENSE COLLECTION
PLUS 2 FREE GIFTS!

YES! Please send me 2 FREE novels from the Suspense Collection and my 2 FREE gifts (gifts are worth about $10). After receiving them, if I don't wish to receive any more books, I can return the shipping statement marked "cancel." If I don't cancel, I will receive 3 brand-new novels every month and be billed just $5.74 per book in the U.S. or $6.24 per book in Canada. That's a savings of at least $2.25 off the cover price. It's quite a bargain! Shipping and handling is just 50¢ per book.* I understand that accepting the 2 free books and gifts places me under no obligation to buy anything. I can always return a shipment and cancel at any time. Even if I never buy another book from the Reader Service, the two free books and gifts are mine to keep forever.

192 MDN EZQ7   392 MDL EZRK

Name _____ (PLEASE PRINT)

Address _____ Apt. #

City _____ State/Prov. _____ Zip/Postal Code

Signature (if under 18, a parent or guardian must sign)

Mail to **The Reader Service:**
IN U.S.A.: P.O. Box 1867, Buffalo, NY 14240-1867
IN CANADA: P.O. Box 609, Fort Erie, Ontario L2A 5X3

Not valid to current subscribers of the Suspense Collection
or the Romance/Suspense Collection.

Want to try two free books from another line?
Call 1-800-873-8635 or visit www.morefreebooks.com.

* Terms and prices subject to change without notice. Prices do not include applicable taxes. Sales tax applicable in N.Y. Canadian residents will be charged applicable provincial taxes and GST. Offer not valid in Quebec. This offer is limited to one order per household. All orders subject to approval. Credit or debit balances in a customer's account(s) may be offset by any other outstanding balance owed by or to the customer. Please allow 4 to 6 weeks for delivery. Offer available while quantities last.

Your Privacy: Harlequin is committed to protecting your privacy. Our Privacy Policy is available online at www.eHarlequin.com or upon request from the Reader Service. From time to time we make our lists of customers available to reputable third parties who may have a product or service of interest to you. If you would prefer we not share your name and address, please check here. ☐

MSUS09HM

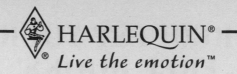

REQUEST YOUR FREE BOOKS!

2 FREE NOVELS
FROM THE ROMANCE COLLECTION
PLUS 2 FREE GIFTS!

YES! Please send me 2 FREE novels from the Romance Collection and my 2 FREE gifts (gifts are worth about $10). After receiving them, if I don't wish to receive any more books, I can return the shipping statement marked "cancel." If I don't cancel, I will receive 3 brand-new novels every month and be billed just $5.74 per book in the U.S. or $6.24 per book in Canada. That's a savings of at least $2.25 off the cover price. It's quite a bargain! Shipping and handling is just 50¢ per book.* I understand that accepting the 2 free books and gifts places me under no obligation to buy anything. I can always return a shipment and cancel at any time. Even if I never buy another book from the Reader Service, the two free books and gifts are mine to keep forever.

193 MDN EZQK   393 MDN EZQV

Name _____ (PLEASE PRINT) _____

Address _____ Apt. # _____

City _____ State/Prov. _____ Zip/Postal Code _____

Signature (if under 18, a parent or guardian must sign)

Mail to **The Reader Service:**
IN U.S.A.: P.O. Box 1867, Buffalo, NY 14240-1867
IN CANADA: P.O. Box 609, Fort Erie, Ontario L2A 5X3

Not valid to current subscribers of the Romance Collection
or the Romance/Suspense Collection.

Want to try two free books from another line?
Call 1-800-873-8635 or visit www.morefreebooks.com.

* Terms and prices subject to change without notice. Prices do not include applicable taxes. Sales tax applicable in N.Y. Canadian residents will be charged applicable provincial taxes and GST. Offer not valid in Quebec. This offer is limited to one order per household. All orders subject to approval. Credit or debit balances in a customer's account(s) may be offset by any other outstanding balance owed by or to the customer. Please allow 4 to 6 weeks for delivery. Offer available while quantities last.

Your Privacy: Harlequin is committed to protecting your privacy. Our Privacy Policy is available online at www.eHarlequin.com or upon request from the Reader Service. From time to time we make our lists of customers available to reputable third parties who may have a product or service of interest to you. If you would prefer we not share your name and address, please check here. ☐

MROM09HM

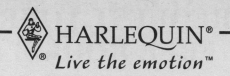

REQUEST YOUR FREE BOOKS!

2 FREE NOVELS PLUS 2 FREE GIFTS!

HARLEQUIN®

Super Romance®

Exciting, emotional, unexpected!

YES! Please send me 2 FREE Harlequin® Superromance® novels and my 2 FREE gifts (gifts are worth about $10). After receiving them, if I don't wish to receive any more books, I can return the shipping statement marked "cancel." If I don't cancel, I will receive 6 brand-new novels every month and be billed just $4.69 per book in the U.S. or $5.24 per book in Canada. That's a savings of close to 15% off the cover price! It's quite a bargain! Shipping and handling is just 50¢ per book*. I understand that accepting the 2 free books and gifts places me under no obligation to buy anything. I can always return a shipment and cancel at any time. Even if I never buy another book from Harlequin, the two free books and gifts are mine to keep forever.

135 HDN EZRV   336 HDN EZR7

Name	(PLEASE PRINT)

Address	Apt. #

City	State/Prov.	Zip/Postal Code

Signature (if under 18, a parent or guardian must sign)

Mail to the **Harlequin Reader Service:**
IN U.S.A.: P.O. Box 1867, Buffalo, NY 14240-1867
IN CANADA: P.O. Box 609, Fort Erie, Ontario L2A 5X3

Not valid to current subscribers of Harlequin Superromance books.

**Are you a current subscriber of Harlequin Superromance books
and want to receive the larger-print edition?
Call 1-800-873-8635 today!**

* Terms and prices subject to change without notice. Prices do not include applicable taxes. Sales tax applicable in N.Y. Canadian residents will be charged applicable provincial taxes and GST. Offer not valid in Quebec. This offer is limited to one order per household. All orders subject to approval. Credit or debit balances in a customer's account(s) may be offset by any other outstanding balance owed by or to the customer. Please allow 4 to 6 weeks for delivery. Offer available while quantities last.

Your Privacy: Harlequin is committed to protecting your privacy. Our Privacy Policy is available online at www.eHarlequin.com or upon request from the Reader Service. From time to time we make our lists of customers available to reputable third parties who may have a product or service of interest to you. If you would prefer we not share your name and address, please check here. ☐

HSR09HM

SPECIAL EDITION™

Emotional, compelling stories that capture the intensity of living, loving and creating a family in today's world.

Desire

Modern, passionate reads that are powerful and provocative.

nocturne

Dramatic and sensual tales of paranormal romance.

Romances that are sparked by danger and fueled by passion.

SDIR07